STRIKER BOY

Striker Boy

Jonny Zucker

Green
Bean
Books

This is a work of fiction and although we'd like it to be true, it just isn't! Everything is made up for your entertainment.

Green Bean Books

Published in 2019 by Green Bean Books,
c/o Pen & Sword Books Ltd,
47 Church Street, Barnsley, S. Yorkshire, S70 2AS
www.greenbeanbooks.com

PUBLISHING HISTORY

Striker Boy was first published by Frances Lincoln Children's Books in 2010. 2Simple published a new edition in October 2017 with all revenue going to good causes including the British mental health charity Mind. This new Green Bean Books edition has extra material by Ivor Baddiel.

ISBN 978-1-78438-544-6

Typeset by JCS Publishing Services Ltd, www.jcs-publishing.co.uk
Printed and bound by TJ International Ltd, Padstow, Cornwall

MIX
Paper from
responsible sources
FSC
www.fsc.org   FSC® C013056

Dedication

For Jonny, a loving husband and father, and for all
those who have been touched by mental health issues.

Contents

In the Net

Nat hit the soccer ball with phenomenal power. The white leather orb flew forward, and thirty thousand seats in the Ivy Stadium slammed shut as the crowd leaped to its feet.

The ball swept around the opponents' wall.

The goalie saw it late. He was the world's number-one keeper—he'd kept a clean sheet for the last twelve matches. He flung his arm desperately, but was no match for the sheer force and placement of the strike. He could only brush a tiny area of the ball's surface with his fingertips before it smashed into the back of the net.

The crowd went crazy; a huge mesh of green and white, arms waving wildly, fists raised aloft, and ecstatic expressions on faces.

The voice of the stadium announcer boomed out from the giant speaker system.

"A goal for Hatton Rangers, scored on thirty-three minutes, by … number nine, Nat Levy!"

Cheers, whistles, and thunderous applause echoed around the stadium.

Nat punched the air with delight, clutched the Rangers logo on his green and white vertically striped shirt, and ran to face the giant bank of spectators. He was a lifelong Hatton Rangers supporter—a local boy made good.

Nat lapped up the adulation and waved his hands, encouraging more. But then suddenly, a single voice cut through the electricity of the moment.

"Nice goal," shouted Nat's dad, "but if we don't get a move on, we'll miss the ferry."

Immediately, the imaginary Hatton Rangers crowd and stadium fizzled into nothingness and Nat was back at the docks of Calais, France.

He waved goodbye to the three French kids he'd been playing with and laughed as they started arguing among themselves about whose turn it was to be goalie next. He grabbed his backpack off the ground and hurried after his dad. They strolled over to the ferry walkway, showed their tickets and were waved on.

Nat stepped onto the walkway and glanced back one last time at French soil. His body jangled with nerves; he was filled with excitement, but also with dread.

After seven years spent traveling the world, he and his dad were finally going home.

2

Past and Present

The ferry journey had been quick and uneventful, and the cab Nat and his dad caught at Dover was heading northward. It was a gray English day in April, with a light wind and the occasional bit of drizzle. Nat gazed at his reflection in the cab window.

Staring back at him was a boy with light-green, almond-shaped eyes, a snub nose, smooth cheeks, a tiny L-shaped dimple on his chin, and long, straight, light-brown hair that fell over his eyes like a curtain. "Is there a face in there?" his dad often joked with him.

Nat was nearly six feet tall and well built, factors that made many people assume he was far older than his thirteen years. In fact he'd only just turned thirteen a few days ago, something he and his dad had celebrated by going out to dinner in Paris, then on to a synagogue, where they'd persuaded the rabbi to bar mitzvah him the following weekend. He glanced across the cab at his dad, Dave Levy, who was looking out of his window, clutching his beloved harmonica.

At least he isn't playing it. Nat smiled to himself.

People often refused to believe that Nat and Dave were related—they looked so different. Dave had much fairer skin. His eyes were cobalt blue and far rounder than Nat's.

His nose was long and thin, he had cropped salt-and-pepper hair, and a permanent scattering of stubble on his face.

As the cab sped on, Nat thought for the millionth time about that terrible February morning seven years ago when his dad had picked him up early from school and told him about Mum's car crash. It had felt like Nat's whole world had caved in and buried him alive. Mum was dead; he'd never see her again.

The funeral was the next day and, after sitting shiva for the rest of the week, they had left England. Dave said they couldn't stay and be haunted by memories of her.

For Nat, the pain of Mum's loss had receded over the years, but he still missed her and thought about her every day, especially on her *yahrzeit*, the anniversary of her death.

In spite of Mum's death, Dave was generally a pretty positive and laid-back kind of guy. But in the last few months, Nat had noticed a change come over him. He had started to look like someone with serious issues on his mind. Things had come to a head a month ago.

"We're going back to England," Dave announced one evening. "I can't keep on dragging you around the world, with no sense of purpose or direction. It's time you got a bit of stability in your life."

Nat was too stunned to speak.

"I've put down a deposit on a cottage I found on eBay," his dad went on. "It needs a bit of fixing up, but we're going to settle down there—make a home."

This sudden cascade of information completely over-whelmed Nat.

On one level he was delighted to be going back to England; he'd be among people who spoke the same language, he'd understand the TV shows, he'd be able to get his favorite chocolate éclair candies, and bagels and lox. And most important of all, it was where Hatton Rangers were based!

But on another level, he felt a deep twist of anxiety in the pit of his stomach. How would he feel returning to the country where Mum had been killed? And besides, he was used to moving on—seeing loads of different places. Settling down sounded so … permanent.

Plus, he and his dad had no family in the UK. Nat's grandparents had died years ago and he hadn't kept in touch with any of his friends from elementary school; he could hardly remember what they looked like. All of Dave's friends had known him through Mum, and he had found it too painful to stay in contact with any of them.

Nat turned to face the window again and watched green fields, farmhouses, and streams passing by. He felt the muggy air in the cab pulling at his weary eyelids and as he drifted toward sleep, he thought of his two favorite subjects—his beloved Hatton Rangers and the year he and his dad had spent in Brazil.

Toxic Arrival

Nat jolted awake as the cab driver applied the brakes. He opened his eyes and saw that they had parked on a stone circle at the top of a narrow driveway. The drizzle had stopped and a few weak rays of sun had appeared.

"The car comes with it," Dave announced, pointing to a battered blue Ford Mondeo slumped in the drive.

Nat took in the vehicle. It looked more like a rust exhibition than a car.

He opened the door of the cab, got out, and stretched his legs. It was then that he saw the white cottage, twenty feet to his left. There was a yellow dumpster outside it.

He made a face. It didn't look like any of the pictures his dad had shown him. For a start, there were several gray tiles missing from the roof. Then there were the numerous windows with no glass. Plus the front door was hanging off its hinges.

Surely this isn't the place. Dad must have gotten it wrong.

Dave looked pretty surprised too.

"Good luck," said the cab driver, turning his car around and heading back down the driveway.

"Let's take a look inside," said Dave, pushing open the front door.

Nat followed. As he stepped into the hallway, the first

thing he saw was a huge mound of yellowing newspapers. It sat beside fragments of a smashed-up wooden desk, a sad sofa sprouting foam, and assorted pieces of broken china and damp wood.

"Uh ... this is the kitchen," said his dad from further down the hallway.

Nat looked inside. The "kitchen" was piled from floor to ceiling with junk; more newspapers, bits of rusty metal, broken chairs, and smashed dishes. The "living room" was exactly the same—another complete garbage dump.

His dad's phrase, "it needs a little fixing up," suddenly felt like the understatement of the millennium.

Together, they climbed the rickety wooden staircase in silence, moving with extreme caution to make sure they didn't fall through any of the gaps. Upstairs were two bedrooms. Both of them contained their own multiple heaps of junk.

"At least the toilet flushes," reported Dave, edging around the mountain of boxes that stood in the bathroom doorway.

"Big deal," replied Nat sarcastically. "It'll take us ten years to fix this place up, Dad, and even then we'll probably want to live somewhere else!"

Dave walked over and put his arm around Nat's shoulders. "Come on, buddy," he said. "Places always look like they're falling down before you start working on them."

"Er ... no, Dad," Nat replied, "this place actually *is* falling down."

"Look, Nat, the nearest town is Lowerbury, which is only about three miles down the road. There's a train station there that goes directly to Hatton Town. Think about it— we've got a direct line to Rangers. We'll go and see them whenever we like."

"Yeah," replied Nat sourly, "as if we'd ever get tickets."

"Of course we'll get tickets. And in terms of the cottage, you'll be surprised at how quickly we'll knock it into shape."

"You think? asked Nat.

"I know." His dad smiled.

Nat gazed up at the shafts of pale yellow sunlight streaming in from the holes in the roof. He stared at the lumps of metal and wood scattered all over the floor.

In his mind this cottage was only good for one thing: immediate demolition.

4

Made in Brazil

"There's something I've got to show you!" said Dave, leading a very despondent Nat back down the stairs.

What? Another mountain of trash?

They went out the front door, turned left and followed a narrow path that passed down the side of the cottage. As they emerged, Nat saw the long wooden porch stretching along the entire back of the cottage. If the wood hadn't been so rotten and splintered it might have been half-decent, but as it was, it looked like it had been constructed from offcuts from the *Titanic* ... after it had sunk.

Nat stepped onto the porch and stared out at the large green expanse of land behind the cottage. It was covered with tall weeds and unkempt grass that stood at least four feet high. At the far end of the field, a small space had been cleared, flanked by two giant oak trees.

"The sellers said they'd sort out the whole field," said Dave with evident disappointment, "but I guess they didn't get around to it."

Nat groaned as he gazed at the jungle in front of them. It would take months to sort this space out, and that was just the yard! This whole project was a total nightmare. How could his dad have bought this place without seeing it? Why hadn't he just waited until they got back to England to buy somewhere? They could have stayed in an Airbnb and come to check this place out properly. When they had seen it, they could have looked for somewhere that didn't need to be condemned.

"It's a great-sized yard, isn't it?" said Dave, trying to sound upbeat. "Why don't we have a kickaround on the flat area by the trees?"

Nat was tempted to refuse and start screaming at his dad for being so incredibly foolish, but the flat patch did look tempting, so he knelt down on the decaying wood of the porch and unzipped his backpack.

It contained a few changes of clothes, basic toiletries, and a John Grisham thriller. He loved thrillers, particularly American ones: Grisham and Harlan Coben were his favorite authors. These weren't the kind of books that your average thirteen-year-old would read, but Nat was different. Because of the independence he'd experienced on the road, and the books and music his dad had introduced him to, he not only looked, but also behaved like a much older person.

His backpack also contained his most prized possession: a scuffed yellow and green ball, bought and battered in Rio. Nat and Dave jumped down off the porch and used their hands to hack their way through the giant grass and weeds. They reached the small, flat area and Nat bounced his ball on the ground. It wasn't England's famous Wembley Stadium, but it would have to do.

It was Nat's dad who had first gotten him into soccer. His mum had tried to get interested in the sport, but it just wasn't her thing. She was much keener on painting and sculpture.

Dave had been an excellent goalkeeper in his time. His hero was Gordon Banks—the goalie who'd won a World Cup winner's medal for England in 1966; the goalie who'd made the "greatest save ever" from Brazilian legend Pelé's header at point-blank range in the 1970 World Cup Finals in Mexico.

Dave had played for his school and county, and, just before his fifteenth birthday, he was offered a tryout at the top English club Chelsea. But the Levy family was in deep financial trouble, so he turned down the tryout and started work as an apprentice carpenter. Nat had asked him several times over the years about this missed opportunity; Dave always said he wasn't bitter about it. Nat wasn't entirely convinced.

Dave was a massive Hatton Rangers fan and introduced Nat to the team when he was little. Nat started listening to Rangers' matches on the radio and, over time, his bedroom walls became splattered with posters and photos of his heroes.

Soon after Nat's fourth birthday, his dad started taking him down to the local park on Sunday mornings to play soccer. Dave taught him how to pass, shoot, and head the ball. Nat was already athletic, and thanks to his dad's coaching, it wasn't long before he could hold his own in school playground matches with boys much older than him.

By the time they left England, six-year-old Nat was a die-hard Hatton Rangers fan and a very decent player.

During the first six months of traveling—in France and Belgium—Nat was too miserable to kick a ball. But gradually he started getting interested again, and from then on he managed to find games wherever they went, from an underground parking garage in Berlin to a dustbowl in Morocco. In all of these matches he picked up tricks and skills.

But it was in Brazil that Nat really learned to play the game. He was eleven and a half when they arrived in Rio de Janeiro. They had intended to stay there for a month or so, but two days after arriving, they found a great second-floor apartment and instantly felt at home. Dave picked up carpentry work easily and Nat accompanied him on several jobs, like he'd been doing for the last couple of years. Whenever Nat wasn't needed on a job, he headed straight for the *praia*—the beach.

Copa Cabana beach played host to people of every skin color and class. They congregated there to relax, enjoy the sun, and play soccer. There was always a game. Sometimes shirts were used as goalposts; other times they had proper beach goals, hired from the lifeguard stations.

In the daytime these games mainly featured kids and teenagers, many of whom were from the poorer neighborhoods, the *favelas*. After sunset, though, when the beach was illuminated with floodlights, and the delicious smell of barbecues wafted through the air, the adults came out, often playing alongside any kids who were still around.

After a couple of days watching these informal matches, Nat plucked up the courage to ask if he could join in. He was welcomed with smiles and nods.

From that moment on, he played soccer on Copa Cabana beach every day. He quickly realized that Brazilians have their own special way with soccer.

He played, he watched, he copied, he adapted. He learned to shield the ball so tightly between his feet that it became almost impossible for an opponent to take it from him. He learned how to lose defenders by rolling the ball at terrific speed, this way and that, with the soles of his sneakers. He learned how to move from a casual stroll to a fierce sprint in a matter of seconds.

When he wasn't at work with his dad or at the beach, he spent hours in their apartment's small backyard, banging a ball against the whitewashed wall, trapping and controlling it—over and over again. Using cans of food as dumbbells, he steadily built up his upper-body strength. He started to look less like a kid and more like a young man.

Twelve months of this intensive Brazilian soccer education turned Nat from a very good player into an exceptional one.

But his time in Rio didn't just transform his soccer

skills. It grabbed his self-confidence and threw it skyward. It instilled in him the belief that out on a soccer field, anything is possible.

And as the days passed, Nat grew more and more certain that becoming a professional player wasn't just his greatest dream. It was his destiny.

5

Target Practice

Dave marched over to the two gnarled oak trees and stood between them. Nat threw the ball into the air. He dipped his head forward and caught it on the nape of his neck.

"Don't be a show-off!" called Dave. "Take a shot!"

Nat flipped his head. The ball flew upward. He let it hit the turf, and then smacked it when it was two feet off the ground. He was Hatton Rangers' striker Robbie Clarke, firing one in at Arsenal's Emirates Stadium.

Dave was up to it. He dived to his left and caught it securely.

"Have another one!" Dave cried, throwing the ball back to him.

This time, Nat controlled it on his chest. He let it bounce twice before he hit it on the half volley. He was now Rangers' brilliant Brazilian winger, Adilson, attacking the West Ham goal at London Stadium. It was an incredibly powerful shot and Dave couldn't catch it. But he did manage to palm it away against one of the trees.

It thudded back toward Nat.

He was determined to score, so he changed tactics.

Instead of going for power, he went for placement. He trapped the ball with the side of his foot and stepped back a few paces. He ran up to the ball as if he were going to place it to his dad's right, but at the last second, dipped his left shoulder and hit it low to Dave's left. Dave dived for it, but he wasn't fast enough. The ball whistled between the trees and flew into a clump of nettles. "*Mazel tov*," said Dave proudly. As a kid, Dave had lived with his Yiddish-speaking grandparents, and he often came out with Yiddish phrases when he was surprised or excited. Nat felt the thrill he experienced every time he scored a goal. He was a center-forward—this was what he was made for.

After that, Nat rifled in shot after shot—varying the pace and position, sending his dad leaping in all directions. His strike rate was about seventy percent, but he wasn't satisfied with that. He kept altering his shooting stance, determined to up his goal count.

After forty-five minutes Dave raised his arms in the air. "Let's call it a day," he said.

"A few more, Dad, go on!" pleaded Nat.

His dad shook his head. "No, it's been a long day; that's enough for today."

Nat was always disappointed when any soccer-related activity came to an end. If it were up to him, he'd play all day and all night, with only the occasional break for a drink. He couldn't get enough of soccer—nothing else came close. It was the only thing that could totally absorb him.

They returned to the back porch and put some newspapers down as seats on the least dank planks. The after-glow of the soccer workout quickly disappeared as Nat's mind returned to the dust shack that was the cottage. Dave reached inside a bag and extracted the cheese sandwiches, bananas, and bottles of Coke he'd bought earlier that day.

He handed Nat his share and they began to eat in silence. Nat stared out at the field, which was darkening by the minute as the sun began to ease down. If they could clear a bigger area, it would be a great place to play, but like everything else around here, that was a giant "if."

"Dad," said Nat, taking a slug from his drink, "why on earth did you buy this place?"

Dave finished his mouthful. "You know why," he replied. "I wanted to give us somewhere solid to start afresh."

"No," replied Nat, "I get that part; it's more about this place in particular. I mean, its rating on the Best Cottages in England website would be well in the minus territory."

Dave put down his bottle and pursed his lips. "I know it looks bad," he admitted, "but every property does if it has been left to decline for years. We'll be able to sort this place out pretty quickly, I'm telling you."

"No way!" snapped Nat. "It's in such a state, we might as well have it knocked down and build something proper in its place!"

"Come on, Nat," said Dave, trying to calm his son, "it's not that bad. I bought it because it has great potential. I think we can turn it into a good home for ourselves. And its biggest selling point was its cost. It was a total bargain!"

Of course it was a bargain—it's worthless!

Nat rubbed his eyes and realized he was grinding his teeth—something he always did when he felt anger building up inside him.

"It's a pigsty," he seethed, "a complete dump, and there's no way we'll be able to turn it around—not this week, not this month, not even this year! We'd need a team of ten people to make it anywhere near habitable! Why did you buy it before we even got a chance to see it?"

Dave's face had that downcast expression that appeared when Nat told him off. He could fight back as coherently as his son, if not more so, when he believed he was right, but on this occasion his face was clearly stating that he knew he might have blown this one.

"Look," said Dave, after a pause, "we're both tired, it's been a very long day, and things always look worse when you see them for the first time. I suggest we talk again in the morning and form some kind of action plan for getting this place into shape."

Nat scowled back at him. It would take a lot more persuasion to convince him that the cottage could ever be a home for them.

"Uh, Dad, how can we go to bed? There are no mattresses or beds, the place stinks and the floors look like they might collapse at any second."

"Don't worry about that," replied his dad, "we're so exhausted we'll get a great night's sleep—no matter what."

6

Practice Makes Perfect

Nat and Dave slept terribly.

They put their sleeping bags down on a small strip of space in the hallway, the location in the house with the fewest rotten floorboards. It was freezing cold, the floor was still filthy and damp, and the fleas feasted on their flesh. The experience gave new meaning to the word "discomfort."

Dave was up early. He changed into his paint-splattered overalls and set to work. After fixing a mezuzah to the front door, he started on the kitchen. He'd bought a huge roll of industrial-strength black garbage bags and by mid-morning there were already three full ones in the dumpster. Nat considered helping, but he was still so furious about his dad buying the place that he avoided the kitchen, grabbed his ball, and returned to the flat section of the yard.

He'd brought a piece of white chalk along—one of those things he'd picked up on his travels but had completely forgotten where. He stood in front of the nearest oak tree and drew three vertical circles on its warped bark. He then stepped back about twenty yards, placed his ball on the ground, and decided on his new challenge. He would have to strike the ball into the top circle five times in a row. If he missed any shots, he'd have to start again. When he'd completed five in the top circle, he'd then move to the middle circle and would need to get five consecutive hits on that one as well. Any misses, and he'd need to start on the middle one again—and the same with the lower one.

He loved setting himself tasks like this. He'd read all about the way England legends David Beckham and Paul Gascoigne had stayed behind after training to work on the accuracy of their shooting and passing. Gazza had spent hour upon hour at the Newcastle training ground, firing a ball through a tire he had hung up. And then of course there was the Blackpool hero, Stanley Matthews, who was so determined to learn to kick with his left foot that he placed his right leg in a splint and ran up and down Blackpool beach, dribbling a ball with his left foot.

Nat spent the whole morning thumping the ball at the circles, pushing himself harder and harder, refining his position and stance, experimenting by shooting with different parts of his foot. He broke for a sandwich and Coke that his dad had driven the mile to the garage on the Lowerbury road to buy.

Dave didn't mention his work on the cottage or Nat's lack of assistance.

Nat spent the rest of the afternoon with his ball and chalk circles and then lay on the grass reading an Ed McBain thriller. Then it was back to shooting practice.

By the time he decided to stop, it was getting dark. He went to inspect his dad's first day of work and was shocked by the scene that greeted him in the kitchen. Despite Dave clearing eleven sacks of garbage, it looked as if the place had hardly been touched.

Supper was another convenience store-bought affair and Nat looked down at his with disdain.

"Are we going to have to eat sandwiches for the rest of our lives?" he demanded, knowing he sounded spoiled but unable to stop himself.

His dad grimaced. "I spoke to the gas and electricity people today. They wouldn't do anything when we were still in France, but now we're back, someone's coming to read both meters on Monday, with a view to turning on the power very soon after. As soon as the gas and electricity are up and running, we'll be having freshly cooked meals."

"I'll believe it when I see it," muttered Nat sulkily.

He chewed at his food without interest and then another thought struck him.

"Where are we going to wash?" he asked.

Dave made a face. "Well … until we … I … can clear the upstairs water pipes we'll have to make do with the stream at the bottom of the back field. I'll have a look at the pipes tomorrow."

"But the water in the stream is freezing!" Nat protested. "We'll die of hypothermia."

"Don't be ridiculous," countered his dad. "A bit of cold water never killed anyone. And anyway, we used a single faucet in the middle of nowhere at that campsite in Norway; I didn't hear you complaining then."

"That's because it was a campsite!" Nat snapped. "Not the place you expect me to call home!"

Dave opened his mouth to reply but thought better of it.

Long after they had finished eating, Nat stayed out on the porch, gazing up at the smattering of stars in the blue-black sky.

What would Mum think about this place if she were here? Would she share my horror or would she get all arty and see it as an opportunity to decorate the place with all sorts of wild paintings and fabrics? Maybe she'd turn the back field into a sculpture yard or something. I could help her set it all up—allowing, of course, for a decent-sized soccer area.

His thoughts then turned to Hatton Rangers. They had a big game against Everton tomorrow and it was vital they got something out of it. On their current form the odds were stacked so heavily against them that only a fool would back them. But that was one of the great things about soccer; you could analyze things until kick-off, but the second a game started, anything could happen.

Changing Life

The following morning, Nat spent some time floating balls into his chalk circles, but his heart wasn't completely in it and his strike rate suffered as a result. He couldn't help feeling badly let down by his dad. Feelings like those didn't go away quickly. When he went back into the cottage at 11 a.m., Dave was just reaching for the car keys.

"I'm heading into Lowerbury," Dave said, "and I'd really like you to come."

"Why?" asked Nat.

"Because I want to buy some stuff for the cottage and you'll say 'I didn't want that one' if I choose anything for you. All you have to do is check out a few shops with me and say yes or no. It's not a big deal."

Nat sighed heavily.

"We'll grab some lunch in a café," Dave offered.

Nat was already halfway out of the door by the time he had finished speaking. He'd do pretty much anything to avoid another sandwich lunch.

The Mondeo spluttered and groaned when Dave turned on the engine, but at least it didn't conk out on the journey. Lowerbury was a mid-sized town, but to Nat's disgust, lots of the stores were old and run-down and there wasn't a sports shop.

What a dump!

They picked up two cheap mattresses, which Dave tied to the roof of the Mondeo, two wooden chairs, soap, shampoo, pillows, cutlery, plates, bowls, a kettle, and a toaster for when (or if) the electricity ever came on.

Following this mini spree they went to the Lighter Bite Café and ordered scrambled eggs and fries for two. Nat savored the food. It was his first proper food for days.

When they'd polished off their meals, including two large slices of apple pie, they allowed themselves one luxury each. Nat bought a family-sized pack of Maltesers. Dave bought a secondhand copy of a sheet music book for the Beatles' *Abbey Road* album, which Nat eyed warily.

So far Dad hasn't played his harmonica, but this doesn't bode well.

They then walked to the far end of the main street and stopped in front of a high brick wall, topped with fencing and bearing a large sign that stated "Burton Comprehensive School." A padlocked iron gate barred the entrance.

"Why are we here?" asked Nat quietly, suddenly dreading the answer.

"I phoned the school administrator a couple of weeks ago," his dad replied. "She said there was a place in your grade so I took up the offer. You start in a couple of weeks."

A couple of weeks! That's so soon you could almost touch it.

Nat hadn't been inside a school for seven years. It was his dad who'd taught him to read, write, and do math. A school was so … so … regimented, so formal and strict. How could he possibly start so soon, when he'd been a free agent for so many years? He gazed up at the building. It looked more like a prison. His forehead wrinkled with apprehension.

"I'll need more than two weeks to settle back into this country," he said firmly. "Why don't I start in September— at the beginning of the next school year?"

"Because," replied his dad, "now we're settling back here, it becomes a legal requirement for you to attend school. This place will give you a proper education—far better than the one I've given you."

"But Dad…"

"Let's leave it for now, Nat," said Dave, sensing another argument.

Nat was miserable on the journey back to the cottage. He felt as if someone had just slammed him inside a giant freezer and locked the door behind them. How could his dad have spoken to the school administrator without telling him?

Back at the cottage, Nat moped around until he saw that it was two o'clock. His eyes suddenly lit up. One hour until Hatton Rangers' game against Everton at Goodison Park. He felt the thrill of anticipation he experienced before every Rangers game. Nat grabbed his worse-for-wear radio and went out onto the back porch. This was a game Rangers couldn't afford to lose—they had to get something out of it.

He knitted his hands together nervously.

Come on, Rangers, don't let me down!

8

The Fixer

Outside Goodison Park—Everton's home ground in the city of Liverpool—a tall, stocky man with piercing blue eyes and thin, unsmiling lips, moved through the crowds. The vast majority of people were making their way into the stadium for the Everton vs. Hatton Rangers game, but he had no intention of entering the ground. His usual beat on a match day was around the Hatton Rangers ground—that was his home turf. But he'd come to Goodison for one thing and one thing only: money.

His name was Tanner and he was known in the underworld as a "fixer"—a man who could get things done, however illegal they might be. Today he was overseeing a network of ticket scalpers—people who bought tickets at face value and sold them on to ticketless fans for vastly inflated prices outside the stadium. Although scalping was against the law and there were plenty of police officers around, Tanner's team of lookouts would give him a tip-off if any of the officers seemed to be taking an interest in the operation.

For Tanner this was a piece of cake; he'd done far bigger jobs in the past and was currently looking for his next big project. He was keeping an eye on his team and mulling over possibilities when his cell phone started ringing. The display said NUMBER WITHHELD.

Tanner frowned. It was a brand-new phone with a brand-new SIM card—he'd only gotten it this morning and had given the number to no one. Could it just be a wrong number?

He pressed to accept the call. "Mr. Tanner," said a deep voice.

"How did you get this number?" demanded Tanner.

"That's irrelevant," said the caller. "Something's come up and I need your help."

Tanner looked around and retreated to a position with his back to one of the stadium walls.

"What kind of something?" he asked.

He listened in silence as the caller outlined his proposition and gave Tanner enough information to prove he was serious about it.

"Would this fall within your field of expertise?" asked the caller.

"Definitely," replied Tanner, whose mind was already working on the plan.

"Good," said the caller, "I want to meet up."

Tanner got out a scrap of paper and a pen and scribbled down the date and time of the proposed rendezvous.

"I'll see you then," said the caller and promptly hung up.

Tanner slipped the piece of paper into his jacket pocket and resumed his overseeing job. The caller's proposal greatly interested him. It was exactly the kind of high-risk, high-stakes project he was looking for.

9

Radio Blues

Nat sat next to the radio, and thoughts of his beloved team's journey over the last few years cascaded into his head.

Hatton Rangers' manager, Ian Fox, had done wonders for the club. When he arrived, the team had just been relegated to the fourth tier and was in danger of leaving the British professional Football Association leagues entirely. After a rocky first season under his management, the team had earned promotion in his second, and five seasons later he'd taken them up to the heady heights of the Premier League. This was their first season with the big boys, but in spite of some solid performances—and a few memorable victories—they hadn't exactly covered themselves in glory. They were presently third from the bottom and in the middle of a desperate fight to avoid relegation.

The radio presenter did a round-up of the other games, getting the views of various ex-players as to what the scores might be. Everyone who was asked about the Rangers game predicted an Everton victory.

What do you all know?

At 2:30, Dave came out to join Nat. They'd talked about the possibility of going to a sports café with cable TV to watch the game, but Nat was quite happy to stay at the house and listen to it. Radio match commentaries had been great companions to him on their travels, even though they'd become more and more nail-biting as Rangers nosedived toward the bottom of the Premier League. The radio let you create your own game-day pictures in your mind—it was a great way to escape day-to-day life.

When they listened to games together, Dave sat in silence with intense concentration on his face. Nat, however, was always on his feet, shouting and gesticulating at the radio.

As 3 p.m. arrived, Nat felt his heart rate increase and his hands go clammy. He was always like this. He lived every pass, header, and shot of every Rangers game.

As had become his custom, he said a little prayer just before kick-off—he didn't know if there was a *bracha* for victory, so he just made one up—but today it seemed to have fallen on deaf ears. Everton came out like a pack of wolves and immediately laid siege to Rangers' goal. After some inspired defending by Rangers captain Neil "the Wildman" Duffy, Everton went ahead in the twenty-first minute. Rangers' center-forward, Steve Townsend, gave the ball away on the halfway line. Everton's Swedish winger, Toni Sondberg, raced down the right wing and squared the ball to his teammate, Charlie Upton, who fired home from close range.

"NOOOO!" Nat yelled at the radio. "It's Townsend's fault; he should never have given the ball away!"

Nat felt jumpy and perturbed for the next twenty minutes or so, but at least Rangers didn't concede again before half-time.

In the fifty-first minute of the second half, Rangers' Brazilian winger, Adilson, struck a beautiful volley from just outside the penalty area. Nat shouted in excitement, willing the ball to go in, but the Everton keeper, Dave Hollick, just managed to push it around the goal post. Steve Townsend then had two good, close-range chances to equalize, but he fluffed them both. Ten minutes before the end, Toni Sondberg went on another of his mazy runs and fired in a low, curling shot that beat the Rangers keeper, Chris Webb.

Nat put his head in his hands. What were the Rangers players thinking of? Didn't they know they were odds-on to go down? Didn't that bother them enough to want to win this match? Wave after wave of Rangers attacks followed, but Everton threw everyone behind the ball and denied Rangers any decent shooting opportunities.

By the time the final whistle went, Hatton Rangers were second bottom of the Premier League. Only Sunderland were below them, by just one point, with Bolton and Wigan above them, two points better off.

Wigan	29 points
Bolton	29 points
Hatton Rangers	27 points
Sunderland	26 points

Nat slumped to the ground next to his dad and flicked off the radio. Rangers couldn't afford to lose any more games.

Eventually Dave stood up and returned to his work in the kitchen. Nat stayed where he was, thinking bitterly about the sorry state in which he found himself.

Rubbish home, rubbish school, rubbish soccer team—can life get any worse?

Five-Minute Cameo

On Sunday morning, Dave announced they were going out in the afternoon.

"Where to?" asked Nat irritably. The only good thing that had happened in the last twelve hours was that they'd each chosen a room last night and slept on their new mattresses. This was a thousand times more comfortable than the floor, but Nat was determined not to show any signs of acceptance that life in the cottage could improve.

And what was his dad offering him now? Another trip to Lowerbury, where he would be reminded of the school he was being forced to go to. *No, thanks!*

But Dave tapped the side of his nose in a "wait and see" gesture. It was a warm day, and the sunshine glinted off windows and other cars' hoods as Dave drove the Mondeo, eventually parking it in a wide residential road. They got out and walked to the front entrance of a big park. Nat gazed up at the huge banner pinned on the park's outer fence: Hatton Rangers in the Community Day.

"It's an apology," Dave said softly. "I know how furious you are with me for buying the cottage, and you've got every right to be. I did it on impulse without really thinking it through. But I promise you, soon it will be a totally different place."

Nat still didn't buy this optimistic outlook, but some of the anger he felt toward his dad dissipated. After all, as surprises went, this was a pretty good one.

The park was a blur of color and movement. A beer tent by the park's entrance was overflowing with people; two ice cream vans were being besieged. On the far end was a play area for younger kids; on the left was a series of vans and stands, selling different types of food; on the right was a long row of trestle tables, piled high with Rangers products and memorabilia.

Nat and Dave spent nearly an hour looking through mounds of Rangers books, magazines, and old DVDs. Nat bought a Rangers vs. Liverpool program from last season. He'd listened to that game on Copa Cabana beach. It had been a thrilling 1–1 tie—one of Rangers' best performances in years. Robbie Clarke had scored with a forty-yard bullet in the last minute to tie the game.

Next they checked out a mini arcade, which boasted some new soccer computer games.

"I like the look of this," said Dave, picking out a game called *Cyber Kick*.

"Wanna try?" asked the stallholder, a skinny boy who didn't look older than ten and was wearing a Rangers shirt that was far too big for him.

Dave nodded enthusiastically.

Nat loved computer games but he wasn't in the mood for them at that moment, so he wandered off, telling his dad he'd see him later. He passed a cotton candy stand, a

Hatton Rangers "Spot the Ball" competition, and a T-shirt stand. At the furthest end of the park was a small concrete soccer court, with white goal lines painted on the fencing.

A group of teenagers, sixteen or seventeen years old, were in the middle of a game—seven vs. seven. One team had their tops on, the others were bare-chested: Shirts vs. Skins. Nat stood outside the fence and watched them. Some of the guys were pretty good and the teams were evenly matched. They must have been playing for quite a while, because when the Shirts netted, someone called out the score: 14–11 to the Skins.

A couple of minutes later, a tall boy with a buzz haircut from the Shirts team went for a fifty/fifty ball and jarred his shoulder against a Skins player's head. He hit the ground awkwardly and winced.

"You all right, man?" asked the kid who'd banged into him.

The tall lad stood up and shook his head. "It kills," he groaned, "I'm gonna sit out for a bit."

He walked toward the gate, pulled it open and stepped past Nat.

A guy from the Shirts team, with a red-and-white bandana on his head, checked his watch.

"We've got five minutes left," he shouted, "and we're a player down. Do you want to play?"

Nat looked over his shoulder expecting someone else to be there, but then realized the question was directed at him.

"Yeah," he called without hesitation.

He ran onto the court, but there was no time to get a feel of the game. The bandana kid passed straight to him, Nat trapped the ball with the sole of his sneaker and flicked it back to the bandana kid, who'd overlapped him. The bandana kid took the ball in his stride and unleashed a screamer that just missed the opposition goal.

A few seconds later, Nat pulled the ball away from a marauding Skins player. The guy stuck his leg out, but Nat jumped over the challenge. He dummied a pass to his right, which sent another Skins player the wrong way, and smacked the ball home with his left instep.

It was a great goal.

14–12 to the Skins.

He clenched his fist in celebration and started running back to his own half. For Nat, there was nothing even close to the elation of seeing a ball crash into the back of the net.

The bandana kid and a couple of the other Shirts players applauded him.

Nat was very involved throughout the next couple of minutes, spraying some excellent passes around and making a brave tackle. He was completely wrapped up in the game.

The Shirts can win this!

A few seconds later, after another Skins attack had been thwarted, the ball came hurtling back toward him. He had his back to goal and could feel a Skins defender right behind him.

He had three options: pass the ball instantly, hold it up and then pass, or get a shot in.

He went for option three.

In one move, he flicked the ball in the air with his left foot, swiveled 180 degrees and hit it with his right foot. It was a thunderous volley.

It bypassed the Skins goalie and flew straight into the goal. The players on both sides stared at Nat with their mouths open.

"Top goal, man!" shouted the bandana kid.

Nat pushed some hair out of his face and muttered "Yesss!" under his breath.

14–13 to the Skins. Come on!

Almost immediately after the kick-off, the ball sailed in Nat's direction again. He took it on his chest and made an inch-perfect twenty-yard pass to the bandana kid, who trapped it cleanly, but scuffed his shot.

Seconds later the game was over. Nat was gutted; his team had lost. Lots of the lads, though, were stunned by Nat's five-minute cameo.

"Who do you play for?" asked the bandana kid, walking over to him.

"No one," Nat replied.

The bandana kid looked at him in surprise. "Well, get yourself a team, dude, you're really good."

Nat laughed and they shook hands. The bandana kid joined the others and they all headed off together, some on foot and some on bikes.

"I saw that volley. It was a blinder! Son, I'm so proud!"

Nat looked up. His dad was standing outside the court.

"Thanks," Nat called, walking over to him. "Did you get battered on *Cyber Kick*?"

"Put it this way"—his dad grinned—"the world of gaming has nothing to fear."

Nat laughed and stepped off the court.

"Want something to eat?" asked Dave. "I'm starving."

"Definitely." Nat nodded.

They had started heading in the direction of the food and drink stalls, when a shadow cut across the path and a tall, imposing figure suddenly blocked their way.

11

The Invitation

A white-haired man with clear blue eyes stood in front of them. He was wearing an old-fashioned raincoat and a peaked gray golfing cap. He had sallow cheeks and a taut, thin body. At first Nat and Dave had no idea who he was, but when he took off his cap they recognized him immediately.

"Aren't you ... Stan Evans?" gasped Nat.

Stan Evans was Hatton Rangers' assistant manager.

"I am, indeed." Evans smiled. "I was just passing through, keeping a low profile, and I happened on your little game. That was quite an impressive performance out there."

Nat's jaw was hanging open. His dad nudged him as a reminder to reply.

"Um ... thanks," said Nat, blushing.

Did the Rangers assistant manager actually just say I gave an impressive performance or am I hallucinating?

"I take it you're a striker?" Evans asked.

"Yes," Nat answered, forcing himself to be less awestruck.

I need to behave like a reasonably sane human being.

"I play center-forward," he continued.

"How old are you, son?"

"Thirteen," replied Nat.

"Thirteen?" said Evans with surprise. "Is he serious, Mr....?"

"Levy," replied Dave, extending his hand, whereupon Evans shook it. "Dave Levy. This is my son Nat and, yes, he is thirteen. It was his birthday a few days ago."

Evans shook Nat's hand.

"Thirteen?" Evans repeated the word thoughtfully. "One of my granddaughters is thirteen and she looks years younger than you. I'd have put you down for sixteen, maybe seventeen."

"He gets it all the time," Nat's dad responded.

Evans nodded his head thoughtfully. "You've got quite a right foot on you, son. That swerve and volley was top drawer. Where did you learn to do that?"

"In Rio," Nat replied.

Evans raised his eyebrows. "What, do you mean *Rio de Janeiro?*"

Nat nodded. "We lived there for a year."

"Really?"

"We've only just gotten back after being away from England for seven years," said Dad.

Evans whistled. "Seven years is a heck of a time," he said. "Have you come back to be with family?"

Nat shook his head. "We haven't got any family here."

"Or even friends," Dave added.

Evans stood there for a few seconds, his mouth twitching, like he was working out some terrifically complex mathematical equation.

"Look," he said, nodding to himself as if he'd just made a decision, "I'd like you to come along for a tryout."

Nat felt a pulse of lightning crackle across his body. "A … a … tryout?" he spluttered. "What … like for Rangers?"

"Yes, son—for Rangers."

Nat cautiously studied Evans's face for a sign that this was a joke. But the assistant manager looked deadly serious. Nat quickly glanced sideways at his dad, who was staring at Evans in amazement.

"Mr. Levy?" asked Evans.

Dave quickly snapped out of his haze. "Yes … I mean … well done, buddy." He slapped Nat on the shoulders. "Of course he'll come."

"Excellent." Evans nodded. "It's Thursday night at the Rangers Academy, right next to the Ivy Stadium. Get there at 7ish for a 7:15 kick-off. Your names will be on the list."

"What, this Thursday?" asked Nat, "In four days?"

"The very one." Evans smiled. "I'll see you then. Don't be late."

He shook both of their hands again and headed off briskly. Nat noticed he walked with a pronounced limp.

Nat and Dave stood in total silence as they watched him disappear into the crowds. It was a good few minutes before either of them was able to formulate anything resembling normal speech.

"*Gott in Himmel,*" whispered Dave.

Nat thought about saying something but chose to remain silent.

"Oh my God" just about covered it.

12

In a Daze

In the car on the way home, Nat was initially in a state of denial: Evans's appearance must have been some sort of daydream, or a program he'd seen on TV, or an idea dropped into his brain by villainous, mind-twisting aliens.

But following this initial burst of uncertainty, the truth slowly began to sink in. Stan Evans, the Hatton Rangers assistant manager, Ian Fox's number two, had invited him—Nat Levy—to attend a tryout at the Hatton Rangers Academy!

How many times had he dreamed about this?

Nat pictured himself at the tryout, running past all ten opposing outfield players before lobbing the keeper with a perfect chip. Next he was scoring a goal from inside his own half. Then he was netting with a majestic diving header from twenty yards.

He was so engrossed in these dreams that his dad's voice gave him a jolt.

"Listen, buddy," said Dave, "I don't want to spoil the party, but please don't get your hopes up too much. The competition at the tryout will be really tough."

Nat fell back to Earth with a thud.

"This is a big time for us," his dad went on. "We've just come home, we're doing up the cottage, you're starting school in a couple of weeks. I don't want anything to knock us off balance."

Nat bristled. "Aren't you pleased for me?" he asked.

"Of course I'm pleased," Dave replied quickly. "It's brilliant. All I'm saying is, try and stay calm."

"OK," Nat replied, "but can I just enjoy the moment?"

"Of course you can," his dad answered, backing off. "You enjoy it. It's great news."

And Nat did enjoy it. He went around for the rest of the day with his head so far up in the sky he felt like he was hovering above the sun. For the first time since they'd arrived back in England, he offered to help his dad with the cottage and Dave accepted. He was so full of joy and excitement that he'd probably have agreed to paint the clouds if his dad had asked him.

"I'm going to nail down some of these loose floorboards. You can start peeling this wallpaper off the kitchen walls," said Dave, delighted to have a partner in his renovation project. "But don't go standing on any rickety chairs to reach the top sections. We don't want you breaking your leg before Thursday night."

Nat worked from late afternoon well into the evening, stripping and peeling the disgusting blue-flecked wallpaper, with questions about the tryout buzzing through his mind. What would the Academy be like inside? Would there be other tryouts on that night? Would they tell him there and then if they wanted him to join the Academy? He'd read a lot about the Rangers youth set-up. They had some excellent coaches and terrific facilities.

But then another thought struck him. Most, if not all, of the other boys at the tryout would have had loads of experience playing for real teams. They'd have had half-decent managers and would have played matches on proper surfaces. They'd be schooled in tactics and strategy. Nat had only ever played in informal kick-arounds. Would this be a major disadvantage?

"Look, buddy," said Dave, after they'd packed up for the night and were munching on two late-night bowls of cornflakes (with milk kept cold in the stream). "About what I said before, on the way back from the Rangers thing."

"What about it?" asked Nat.

"I didn't want to put a downer on things. It's just that … if they don't ask you back after the tryout, it could knock you badly. I just want you to approach this with a little bit of caution. You're my son. I want to give you some protection."

Nat nodded. "I know that and I'm trying not to freak out. But come on, Dad. This is a tryout for Hatton Rangers! It's the best thing that's ever happened to me."

"Of course it is." Dave smiled, glancing at his watch. "It's absolutely fantastic. But you need all the rest you can get so let's hit the hay."

"Cool," agreed Nat.

Fifteen minutes later, they both turned in for the night. Nat was completely exhausted from the day's drama and he fell asleep with the words of Stan Evans still ringing in his ears.

13

Surreal

How Nat got through the next three days, he had no idea. He'd never felt so anxious or excited about anything before—nowhere even close. He spent all of his time alternating between helping his dad in the kitchen and training. He went for several long runs down the Lowerbury road. He did push-ups and sit-ups and stretches. And he spent hours smashing his ball against the chalk tree circles, refining and honing his skills and concentrating fiercely.

When it came to the cottage, he started to see some shoots of improvement. On Monday evening, they finally cleared the last pile of junk from the kitchen—the dumpster was now completely full and Dave said he'd phone the dumpster company in the morning to order an exchange. On Tuesday, the gas was switched on, so Dave spent most of the day uncovering and unblocking the ancient radiators. And on Wednesday morning, Dave managed to unblock the last of the pipes, which allowed clean water to flow into the shower unit. It was a joy after washing in the stream to take a shower, even if the hot water only lasted five minutes.

On Wednesday afternoon, the electricity came on and Nat and his dad began work on the sitting room. Dave made several quiet comments about things "coming together," but he didn't push it. He knew that Nat was still angry with him and he wasn't going to have any celebrations until the whole place was spick and span.

The tryout was constantly on Nat's mind and even when it wasn't taking center stage it was waiting in the wings. One hour! That's how long the tryout would last. One hour to convince the Rangers coaches he had what it took to become a member of the Academy. If he managed to display his talents, they might ask him to join the Academy and if they did, maybe he could work his way up through the youth teams, play for the reserves, sign professional terms when he was sixteen! But if he played badly … the thought was unbearable.

On Wednesday night he dreamed he was at the tryout, but while other players were wearing AstroTurf cleats, he was sporting enormous, fluffy dinosaur slippers. He could only move very, very slowly, and even when he did get near the ball, he couldn't summon enough power in his dinosaur feet to kick it.

14

Pitch-side Panic

Nat woke up the next day and lay in silence for a few moments, looking up at the damp ceiling in his room.

And then it suddenly hit him. It was Thursday, the day of the tryout—the biggest day of his life!

He found his dad in the kitchen, drinking a cup of strong black coffee.

"You all right?" Dave asked, looking up.

Nat smiled weakly. 'What are we up to today?' he asked.

"That's the spirit, buddy." Dave winked. "Working will take your mind off the tryout. Have something to eat and then we'll clear some more of the living room."

"Cool," Nat replied, the nerves bubbling furiously inside him.

It was only 9 a.m. He had ten hours to get through. The day crawled badly. Nat tried not to let the pressure of the tryout overwhelm him, but he couldn't stop it.

Tonight could be the start of his entire future. He practiced shooting in the field, and he helped his dad carry and then chuck some huge chunks of wood and metal into the dumpster. But all the while his nerves were vibrating with tension … and fear.

At 5 p.m. Dave said it was time to pack up and Nat felt the nerves crank up a gear. Dave prepared a supper of bread, cheese, and apples. Nat had no appetite, but he knew he had to take on some fuel. At 5:50 they drove to Lowerbury station.

On the train Nat couldn't keep still. He drummed his fingers on his knees and tapped his feet up and down on the carriage floor. Thoughts circled around inside his brain like greedy vultures.

What if I play badly? What if all the other lads get through and I don't? What if … What if … What if?

"Try and relax, buddy." His dad smiled.

"I can't," Nat muttered.

Dave squeezed his shoulder. "It's good you're nervous—shows the adrenaline's kicking in."

There was a light drizzle when they emerged from Hatton Town station at 6:30. The sun was just emerging from behind a cloud and it wouldn't be dark for a couple of hours. All around them people were hurrying by, briefcases, umbrellas, and shopping bags swishing. As they turned the corner into Grange Road, the Ivy Stadium suddenly appeared. The Shipper End rose above them, its rows of green and white seats neatly stacked above each other.

Nat gazed up in awe.

He and his dad had driven past the stadium a few times when he was younger, but to be here for a tryout was incredible. The Academy was right next to the stadium and they reached the security barrier at 6:40. The guard checked their names on his list, took digital photos of them, and attached the photos to their security passes. They walked about fifty yards down a path and then went through a set of giant glass double doors.

As soon as they entered the dome-shaped heart of the Academy, the noise hit them like a bullet train. The dome's steel roof glimmered in the bright floodlights. Green AstroTurf carpeted the entire floor. The walls carried the faint impressions of a million balls, smashed against them by players eager to impress. The dome smelled of stale sweat and nervous breath.

There were obviously quite a few tryout games tonight, because some of them had already started. About ten yards in was a temporary signpost. Nat counted the games on it. There were eight in total.

His nerves cranked up another notch.

He and his dad followed a sign pointing to the under-fourteens game.

But as they neared the pitch, they saw that something was wrong—badly wrong. Stan Evans had told them to be here at 7ish for a 7:15 start.

It was only 6:55.

But the under-fourteens game had already kicked off.

15

Out of Position

There were two teams battling it out on the under-fourteens field: one in orange bibs, the other in yellow.

"Excuse me," said Dave, approaching a bearded guy who was standing on the sidelines staring at a clipboard. "But do you know when this match kicked off?"

"About ten minutes ago," the man replied without looking up.

"Well, where are the other under-fourteens games?" asked Nat.

"There aren't any."

You can't be serious! This is the most important match of my life and it has already kicked off!

Nat and Dave stared at each other with bewilderment, but before they could say anything further, Stan Evans appeared. "Evening, gentlemen," he greeted them with a warm smile. "Welcome to Rangers. What I'd like you to do is…"

"This game's already started," said Dave, cutting Evans off.

Evans nodded. "Nat isn't going to play in this game tonight," he replied, pointing to the far side of the dome. "He's playing over there."

Nat relaxed a tiny bit. The bearded guy had got it wrong. There must be another under-fourteens game. He crossed the dome with his dad and Evans, looking all around him at the mass of players trying to prove they were good enough to join the Academy. But his relief at heading for the right tryout was only momentary. The sign on the sidelines of the field Evans stopped at read "under-seventeens."

"Um … this is the under-seventeens," said Nat uncertainly.

"This is where I want you to play tonight," replied Evans.

Nat and Dave gaped at Evans in shock. "You're joking, right?" said Dave.

Nat stared at the boys on the pitch warming up. They mostly looked sixteen and there were some serious muscle-heads out there.

"But … but … they're all miles older than me," he spluttered.

"That didn't seem to matter on the court at the 'Rangers in the Community' day, did it?" said Evans.

Nat swallowed hard. That was true, but this was a tryout. Surely it was only fair if he played with boys his own age.

"I know it's unusual, but I want you both to go with me on this one," said Evans.

Nat gazed at him in disbelief.

"Oh, and there is one other thing," added Evans. "I want you to play right-back."

"WHAT?" Nat blurted out.

Joining the under-seventeens game was very worrying, but playing right-back? How could he show off his skills as a center-forward if he was playing in defense?

"I know it's not your usual position," said Evans,

trying to allay Nat's anxiety, "but there are a lot of lads to accommodate tonight and I need you to play there."

"This is ridiculous!" exploded Dave. "Nat's not some kind of experiment, Mr. Evans. There's no way he's playing in this game!"

"I understand your concerns," replied Evans calmly, "but I have Nat's best interests at heart. Please trust me."

"You haven't got his best interests at heart!" seethed Dave. "If you had, you'd have told us to get here earlier and Nat would be playing in the under-fourteens!"

Nat shared his dad's confusion and fury, but there was something about the expression on Stan Evans's face that made him suddenly freeze. It was his ice-cool determination; he looked completely and utterly sure of himself and that struck a chord deep in Nat.

"I'm going to play," Nat announced quietly.

His dad spun around to face him. "What?"

"I said I'm going to play."

Dave's mouth opened and closed several times like a little kid blowing bubbles. "I think this is a really bad idea," he counseled.

But Nat was already crouching down on the floor and getting his jersey out of his backpack. He pulled on his old green-and-white Rangers shirt, and white Rangers shorts. He kicked off his shoes and laced up his AstroTurf sneakers—the ones they'd picked up cheap in Spain.

"It feels all wrong," muttered Dave.

But Nat filtered his dad's words out of his head. Of

course he'd prefer to play center-forward in the under-fourteens, but Stan Evans was the Rangers assistant manager, not Dad. If Evans wanted him to play right-back in the under-seventeens, then that's what he was going to do. It was a tryout for Hatton Rangers, for heaven's sake. He'd play goalie if Evans asked him to!

The boys warming up on the pitch were passing, juggling, and firing balls into the empty nets. Nat stood up and did some stretches.

Dave was wringing his hands. "Please, Nat, think about this," he said.

Nat turned and did a couple of short runs in the opposite direction.

A tall, thin referee, dressed in black, appeared on the field, holding a whistle and carrying an armful of blue and red bibs.

"We're starting in two minutes," he called out, "so listen out for your names."

"Please, Nat," his dad repeated.

But Nat was in the "zone"—the private mental place he always entered prior to a match. He heard his name being called out. He was playing for the Blue team.

Dave grabbed his elbow and looked at him anxiously. "You don't have to do this," he urged, anxiety rippling over his face.

"I do," Nat replied, shaking his elbow free.

He looked back for a second at Stan Evans, took a deep lungful of air, and ran onto the field.

16

Shattered Dream

Half an hour later, Nat would have happily killed Stan Evans.

He'd touched the ball three times in the entire first half, and each of these touches had just been a short pass. The Reds were a far better team than the Blues and almost all of the action had been on the other side of the field. The Red right-winger had run rings around the Blue left-back; he'd made a goal apiece for each of the Red strikers and had netted one himself.

The Academy will sign him up, thought Nat bitterly as the ref blew his whistle for half-time.

Nat traipsed off the field, cursing himself for not listening to his dad. He slumped onto one of the orange plastic chairs on the sidelines, hot tears of anger and frustration welling up behind his eyes. What the heck was Evans thinking—playing him at right-back in the under-seventeens tryout? Forget about getting a place at the Academy, forget about moving up through the ranks, forget about ever becoming a professional soccer player. His whole life plan had just been shattered by those thirty terrible minutes. How could Evans do this to him?

"This stinks." Dave spat out the words furiously as he hurried to Nat's side.

His whole face was red. "You're by far the youngest lad out there, you're playing out of position, and the Reds have a monopoly of the better players. How can you impress anyone in that situation? When Stan Evans shows up, I'm going to give him a piece of my mind."

At that second, Stan Evans did show up.

"I want you both to forget about the first half," he said quickly, trying to take the sting out of Nat and Dave's fury.

"How are we supposed to do that?" Nat demanded miserably. "I suppose you're going to play me at left-back in the second half so that that Red right-winger can skin me?"

"Look, Mr. Evans," said Dave, forcing himself not to shout. "You said to trust you and we trusted you. But look what happened. I want Nat to play in the under-fourteens for the rest of the evening."

Evans sighed deeply. "Firstly, the under-fourteens game is almost finished," he replied. "Secondly, Nat's going to be playing center-forward for the second half of this game."

This news injected a tiny drop of hope into Nat's mind, but he still felt crushed by his terrible first-half performance.

"That doesn't solve the problem of him playing in the under-seventeens," Dave hissed.

"I'll tell you what," said Evans, stroking his chin. "Let's see how Nat does in the second half. If he doesn't get the chance to show his true abilities—because of the age gap—I'll invite him to the next tryout night and he can play the whole game in the under-fourteens. How does that sound?"

Nat took a deep breath and thought about it. However much he hated Evans at that moment, this did seem like a reasonable proposition.

Dave prodded the toe of his right shoe into the ground.

"I'll do it," Nat mouthed at him.

"OK," conceded his dad reluctantly, "if Nat's up for it, then that's what we'll do. But I'll hold you to that promise, Mr. Evans."

"You have my word," replied the assistant manager.

That moment, the ref blew his whistle to summon the players for the second half.

Evans fixed his gaze on Nat. "Treat the second half like a brand-new game," he said with an encouraging smile. "You'll do well."

Nat stood up.

Despite agreeing to stick with this game, somehow he didn't quite share Evans's optimism.

17

Showcase

There had been a lot of changes at half-time and the teams were now far more evenly matched. Nat was playing up front for the Blues with a wiry boy with mini dreadlocks called Danny.

It only took a couple of minutes before the Blues got their first proper chance of the game—Danny headed a cross just wide of the Red goal.

"Unlucky," Nat called.

Following that, Nat made a couple of decent passes and slowly felt the disappointment beginning to ease off a little. A few minutes later, a Red striker was standing on the half-way line looking for options, when Nat snuck in and nabbed the ball. The striker aimed a kick at Nat, catching him on the back of his left calf. Nat wobbled, but kept his balance. Danny sped past him and Nat rolled the ball toward him.

Running forward, Nat took the return pass from Danny. He charged past two Red defenders and entered the penalty area. The keeper ran out to narrow the angle. Nat could have shot—and might have scored—but Danny was in a better position. So, dummying a shot with his left foot, he flicked the ball sideways with the outside of his right boot. It spun toward Danny, who curled it first time into the top left corner of the net.

"Great goal!" shouted Nat, slapping Danny on the back.

"Great pass!" replied Danny, grinning.

Nat glanced over and saw his dad raising his hands above his head and clapping enthusiastically. He felt a few sparks of confidence ignite inside him.

As the second half progressed, Nat got more and more possession and struck some strong and accurate passes, including an excellent cross-field one to the lad on the right wing. He also had two very good attempts on goal: a fierce right-foot volley that was saved brilliantly by the Red goalie, and a superb, curling free kick from thirty yards that narrowly missed the left post.

The Blues dominated the second half, and three minutes before the end Nat had a diving header parried by the Red keeper. His spirits were soaring and he was desperate to get as much possession as possible. The score remained 3–1 to the Reds—until the dying seconds of the game.

The ref had just checked his watch when Nat received a pass ten yards inside his own half. He looked up and saw the Blue right-winger speeding down the sideline. Nat hit him an inch-perfect pass and began to run through the field's central channel. The winger took the ball in his stride and darted past the Red left-side midfielder. Nat continued his run. The winger clipped the ball infield to Danny, who stroked it on to Nat.

Nat sensed one of the Red center-forwards running

toward him. He waited a second and then pushed the ball to the right of the advancing player. The kid was going too fast to change direction. Nat stepped out of his way and scooted past him, picking up the ball up on his other side.

Danny called for the ball to his right. Nat tapped it sideways and sprinted forward. Then he saw the Red left-back hurtling toward him. He was twenty-five yards away from the Red goal. Danny took a step forward with the ball.

Nat hung back a second, making sure he was parallel with the Red left-back. Danny saw what he was doing, waited a couple of seconds, then lofted the ball over the head of the left-back. In that split second, Nat sprang forward. He felt the left-back's body clattering against his, but he used his momentum to shrug him off with his left shoulder and powered past him. As the ball descended, Nat took it on the chest. The Red left-back tugged desperately at Nat's shirt, but he hardly made any impact. The ball hit the turf and bounced. It arced upwards and Nat smacked it on the half volley.

As soon as his shoe connected he knew it was a sweet strike.

The Red keeper dived. For a second, it looked as though he would divert the ball around the post with his fingertips, but it flew past him and smashed into the back of the net.

Nat raised his fists in the air. Any last traces of despair

vanished with that shot. He'd just scored a fantastic goal in a tryout match for Hatton Rangers!

"Amazing goal!" shouted Danny—running over and jumping on Nat's back. Nat laughed. Dave was clapping thunderously on the sidelines. The Red keeper furiously picked the ball out of his net and booted it up toward the center circle. A few of the Blue players shouted congratulations to Nat, but several held back. They didn't want to give him too much attention—they were still on tryout themselves.

As Nat and Danny took the kick-off, the ref blew for full-time.

Nat went around shaking hands with all of the players. The ones who had done well were all smiles. The others scowled at him sourly.

The ref then called everyone to the center circle. "Well done, lads," he said. "There were some decent performances out there tonight. The club will contact you sometime next week."

Nat and Danny trooped off the field together. "Got to go," Danny said, pointing to an older boy of about nineteen, standing on the sidelines. "Can't keep my brother waiting."

"Maybe see you again," Nat shouted.

"Yeah," Danny called back, "when we're the Rangers forward line!"

Nat laughed and walked over to his dad, who stood beaming on the sidelines.

"I'm so proud of you! You were amazing! I'm *shlepping* such *nachas*!" Dave exclaimed, grabbing him and giving him a bear hug.

"Easy, Dad!" laughed Nat.

He broke away from his dad's grasp and savored the moment. Maybe playing in the under-seventeens hadn't been such a bad thing after all. Perhaps Evans had wanted him to prove himself among older players, so that he stood a better chance of convincing Rangers to take him on at the Academy. Whatever the reason, he was delighted with his second-half performance and ecstatic about scoring such a great goal.

Stan Evans walked over. "You see," he said, smiling. "I told you the second half would be different."

"He wasn't bad, was he?" Nat's dad grinned proudly. "But I still don't know why you wanted him to play in the under-seventeens, and the thing is…"

The ringing of Evans's phone cut Dave short. "Excuse me for a second, gentlemen," Evans said, and walked some distance up the sidelines to take the call. "They'll tell us next week if we're through," Nat said.

"I'm sure they'll ask you back," his dad said. "They'd be mad not to! You were outstanding in the second half, and as for that goal…"

Nat pulled on his sweatshirt and swapped his sneakers for shoes.

"Well, it's been an amazing evening," Dave said, picking up Nat's bag. "Let's go home."

To their right, Evans was still on his cell.

"Bye, Mr. Evans," Nat shouted, and he and his dad waved at the Rangers assistant manager.

Evans motioned with the palm of his hand for Nat and Dave to stop.

"Can you two hang on for a minute?" he called over. "There's someone I'd like you to meet."

18

The Set-up

Less than a mile away from the Rangers Academy, a large, black, expensive station wagon snaked its way up to the sixth and top floor of a parking garage. Its windows were tinted; its gleaming hubcaps caught the reflection of the garage's low-level lighting. The car's ascent was smooth and almost noiseless thanks to the efficiency of its powerful engine. It emerged slowly around the last bend. Twenty yards away, a 4x4 was parked in a bay. The station wagon paused for a second, as a hunting animal might before making its move. Then it glided slowly toward the parked vehicle and pulled into an empty space ten yards away.

The engine was cut and the station wagon's driver climbed out, strode around to the back of the car, and pulled open a door.

No one emerged.

The driver stood silently beside the door. His eyes swept across the vicinity. There were a handful of other cars parked up here but none of their drivers were around, apart from the one behind the wheel of the 4x4. The driver glanced over to a mounted CCTV camera and nodded with satisfaction. It hadn't cost him much to get the night security guard to deactivate the camera that focused on this particular section of the sixth floor.

Tanner—the 'Fixer'—was at the wheel of the 4x4. He watched the station wagon and its motionless driver for a few moments, then flicked open his door and got out. The parking

63

garage smelled of oil and grease. Looking instinctively over his shoulder, Tanner strode over to the station wagon. The driver nodded at Tanner, but his face was completely devoid of emotion. Tanner stooped and climbed inside the car. The driver closed the door behind him.

The car was roomy inside, with plenty of space for a state-of-the-art multi-media player and surround-sound speakers. The man in the back was in his sixties, with a graying ponytail, thin lips, and a diamond stud in his left ear. He was known to all of his associates as Mr. Knight. That was what it said on his passport and on a wide range of other identification documents he possessed.

But it wasn't his real name.

He hadn't used his real name for over thirty years.

No one, not even his most trusted lieutenants, knew it.

Knight was dressed in an immaculate charcoal-gray, three-piece designer suit and slim, dark glasses that shielded his eyes.

"Mr. Tanner." Knight nodded by way of a greeting. "I'd like your opinion on the matter I mentioned on the phone."

Tanner inclined his head.

Knight reached into an inner pocket and withdrew a piece of paper bearing the names and profiles of the sixteen Hatton Rangers players who made up the core of the club's first-team squad. Three players were circled in blue ink; the rest were crossed out in red. Knight handed the list and a red pen to Tanner.

"Your thoughts on these three?" asked Knight coolly.

Tanner studied the list for less than a minute. He took the pen and drew a red line through two of the blue-circled names. Then he handed the paper and the pen back.

"*Are you sure about this?*" demanded Knight, his head inching forward, looking at the one remaining player's name.

"*Absolutely,*" replied Tanner.

Knight nodded with satisfaction. "*Good,*" he continued. "*From this point on, your remit is to deal with the player. I'll line up the investors.*"

"*Agreed.*"

"*This is a small contribution to your set-up costs,*" said Knight, handing over a bulging white envelope. Tanner slit it open and saw a huge bundle of fifty-pound notes. He tucked the envelope into his pocket.

Knight stared at him for a few moments and then pressed a black button on his armrest. "*Mr. Tanner and I have concluded our business,*" he announced.

Five seconds later there was a click and the door was pulled open by Knight's driver.

"*Let's speak soon,*" said Knight.

"*I'll be in touch,*" replied Tanner.

There was no further goodbye, no handshake; it was strictly business. Tanner eased out of the car and before he'd fully stood up, the driver had closed the door behind him.

All sign of Knight disappeared. Tanner strode back across the asphalt and as he did so, he heard the black station wagon start up. He climbed into the 4x4 and watched the other car glide toward the exit ramp and disappear from view.

He waited for a couple of minutes and then started the 4x4's engine.

19

Mystery Man

"This way please, gentlemen."

Stan Evans pushed open a set of large wooden double doors at the far end of the dome. He led Nat and Dave up two flights of stairs. On the second floor, they walked out onto a plushly carpeted hallway. Tiny but powerful spotlights every couple of yards gave the place a kind of futuristic, spaceship feel.

"We're crossing over to the stadium now," Evans informed them. "The buildings are linked by this hallway."

"This place must have cost a fortune," whispered Dave.

Nat had no idea where they were going, or who they were going to meet, but he assumed it was someone from the Rangers youth set-up. At least he hoped it was. Maybe Evans had been so impressed by his second-half performance that he was going to sign him up for the Academy tonight. It seemed too good to be true, but you never knew.

Each door Nat passed had a name and a job title, like "Mike Tench—Junior Rangers" and "Helen Aldershot—Publicity." The corridor walls were covered with photos of current Rangers players. There was Neil 'the Wildman' Duffy beside Adilson, who was next to Kelvin Bartlett. Interspersed with these were pictures of Rangers' celebrity supporters wearing the club jerseys.

He drank in every image. If he never came here again, at least he'd have the visuals committed to memory.

Evans finally stopped outside a black door on the right, at the far end of the hall. He knocked twice.

"Come in," boomed a deep voice from inside.

Evans opened the door and ushered them inside. They found themselves in a large boardroom with a huge, oval, mahogany table as its centerpiece. The table's surface had been polished so vigorously it almost blinded them. High-backed brown leather chairs flanked the table. A majestic chandelier hung from the ceiling. Adorning the walls were paintings of famous Rangers matches from each stage of the club's history.

Across the table, someone was sitting with his back to them. His chair suddenly spun around and a very familiar face greeted them.

"Good evening, gentlemen." He nodded. "I'm Ian Fox—the Hatton Rangers manager."

20

The Offer

Nat gaped at the Rangers manager in utter shock.

Fox was in his mid-forties. He had short black hair streaked with gray at the sides, and it was longer at the back. It wasn't exactly a seventies hairstyle, but it was dangerously close. He had a sharp, angular nose, thin lips, and shiny brown eyes. On his left cheek was a three-dotted scar—reminiscent of traffic lights.

Nat's mind was racing. He knew from the press that Fox took a keen interest in the club's Academy, but surely the manager left the under-fourteen players to the youth team coaches—even if one of them had just played a blinding second half in an under-seventeens tryout?

"Please, sit down," Fox beckoned them over.

Nat glanced sideways at his dad, who looked as shocked as Nat felt. They both sat while Evans walked around the table and perched next to Fox.

"You must be wondering why we've asked you up here," Fox began.

"Um … yes," Nat replied uncertainly.

Fox placed the palms of his hands flat on the table. "There are only five more games this season," he began, "and Rangers are odds-on to go down. Many of our players have lost their confidence; some are in danger of losing their dignity."

Nat stared at Fox, still trying to take in the fact that he was sitting in the same room as the Rangers manager. "Relegation would be a disaster for us," Fox went on. "We'd lose all of our money from Premiership TV rights and we'd fall into very serious financial difficulties."

Nat nodded. This wasn't earth-shattering news—it was the fate of every club facing the drop.

"Unfortunately, though"—Fox winced—"the picture's even worse than that."

Nat and Dave frowned simultaneously.

"If we do go down"—and here Fox lowered his voice— "our chairman, Steve Pritchard, is going to pull out of the club. He's already put millions into us and he's not prepared to fund a team in the second tier. If Pritchard goes, Rangers go. The club will go bankrupt—we will cease to exist."

Nat was horrified. Rangers ceasing to exist? That would be like waking up one morning and discovering the sky had vanished.

"Sorry, Mr. Fox," said Dave slowly, "that's appalling news, but I can't see what it's got to do with us. I mean, I don't want to be rude or anything, but surely you don't meet every post-tryout kid and give him an exclusive update on the club's potential demise?"

Fox leaned across the table conspiratorially, his eyes darting from Dave to Nat.

"This gentleman here," said Fox, indicating Stan Evans with his thumb, "knows more about soccer than anyone else I've ever met. He came back from the 'Rangers in the Community' day raving about this kid he'd seen on the soccer field. He said the kid was thirteen but totally outclassed a group of much older lads."

Nat looked at Fox in wonder.

Is he talking about me?

Fox quickly turned his gaze on Dave. "I watched the second half of the under-seventeens game tonight, Mr. Levy, and I saw pretty quickly that Nat is a bit of a special player. Just like Pelé, just like Best, just like Maradona—your lad has natural, raw talent. Finding players who possess that kind of quality is the holy grail of the soccer world."

Nat blushed deeply.

Did the Hatton Rangers manager really just mention my name in the same breath as three of the world's all-time greatest players?

Dave shuffled uncomfortably in his chair. Unlike Nat, these comparisons seemed to unsettle him.

Fox cleared his throat. "Stan told me you've only just returned to England, after being away for seven years. Is that right?"

Nat and Dave nodded.

"He also said you have no friends or family in England. It's almost like … the two of you don't exist."

Dave scratched his ear. "What are you getting at, Mr. Fox?"

"Let me get straight to the point," said Fox. "The transfer window closed ages ago and even if it hadn't, I don't have any more money to spend; I've tried all of our promising reserve players, I've taken lads on loan, I've even called in some semi-retired players to see if their experience can do the trick. But nothing has worked. I'm a desperate man and that calls for desperate measures."

"What kind of measures?" asked Dave, his brow furrowing.

"Nat could easily pass for sixteen, or older," said Fox. "If no one knows him, no one knows his age. And if no one knows his age, then what's to stop him actually playing for this club?"

Fox's words shot through the air like fiery cannonballs.

Dave opened and closed his mouth. Nat gaped at the Rangers manager, expecting him to suddenly burst out laughing, as a hidden camera crew jumped out of a cupboard, declaring him to be the latest victim of some TV show prank.

"You're joking, aren't you?" whispered Nat.

"No, Nat," Fox replied with a resolute expression, "I'm completely serious."

For a few seconds no one spoke. The tension in the room was so thick you could have cut it into slices.

"Let me get this straight," said Dave, eyeing the Rangers manager carefully. "You want to tell the world that Nat is sixteen so that he can play for Rangers—the real Rangers, not the youth team?"

"Precisely." Fox nodded, his eyes sparking with a film of excitement and hope.

"You're planning to place the entire responsibility of saving this club on my thirteen-year-old son?"

"No," Fox shot back, "of course not; all I'm saying is that I'd do anything to save this club, and I believe Nat could possibly play a part. It may turn out that he isn't good enough or strong enough or quick enough to get anywhere near the first team; he may pick up an injury—anything could happen. But Stan and I are convinced Nat's good—very good. And if he's good enough, he's old enough."

Nat's body crackled with electricity. "Unreal," he mouthed in amazement.

This is the greatest moment of my life! It's unbelievable. Fox wants ME to join Rangers!

There then followed a deathly silence. It was Dave who eventually broke it. "I hope Rangers survive," he said quietly, "I really do. I've supported this club my whole life and I don't envy your situation at all, Mr. Fox. It's a complete nightmare."

"Yes." The Rangers manager nodded, hanging on to Dave's every word.

"But the answer is no."

Nat felt a sharp stab of pain in his chest. Fox's face crumpled. Evans winced as if someone had just punched him.

"I know it's a very extreme measure," said Fox croakily, "and I understand that you want to shield your son—I have two boys myself, Mr. Levy; one of them is Nat's age. But I really believe we can make this work."

"You mean save your skin," hissed Dave, jabbing a finger at Fox.

"No, this isn't just about my survival," countered Fox.

"It's about Rangers' survival. And not only that—I really think Nat could benefit from this as well. He's already a very promising player. Think of what he could become with the kind of coaching and mentoring we could offer. All we need to do is add three years onto his age."

"Well, I think the way this whole evening has panned out is pretty disgraceful." Dave seethed. "First you put Nat into the under-seventeens game without telling us why, and now you tell us about this … this … absurd scam. I'm sorry, but it's completely out of the question."

"But, Dad…" ventured Nat, thinking his brain was about to explode.

"No, Nat," snapped his dad, standing up and shaking his head dismissively. "I can't have your head filled with this rubbish."

Fox stood too, and quickly reached into his pocket. "Please, Mr. Levy—at least think about this offer after the initial shock has worn off. You can phone me at any time—my numbers are all there."

Dave hesitated for a few moments and then reluctantly reached out his hand and took Fox's card.

"I won't be changing my mind," he muttered. "Come on Nat, we're going home."

Nat stood up numbly, his body and mind shattered by the intense scene that had just been played out. As they stepped back into the hallway, one overwhelming thought hammered inside his head.

Thanks a lot, Dad—you've just ruined my life.

21

Numb with Shock

Nat stared out the window on the train home; the silhou-
ettes of factories and houses flashed by as drops of light
rain clung to the carriages. His entire body felt cold and
numb. Blurred images of the night's events sped around
inside his head and collided with one another. What should
have been a triumphant evening had ended with a very
bitter twist and a feeling of crushed disappointment.

Dave's expression was drawn and upset. "Fox was really
out of line tonight," he snarled, glancing anxiously at
his son. "I mean, what does he think he's doing—asking
a thirteen-year-old to save his club? It's a disgrace! I'm
tempted to call the papers in the morning and tell them
about Fox's little proposition."

But Nat couldn't drag his gaze away from the window.

This can't be happening to me. It's just a bad dream.

"Anyway," said Dave, trying to inject a brighter note into
his voice. "You impressed them and that was the whole
point, wasn't it? They'll definitely give you a place at the
Academy. You can go there after school and on weekends.
It will be great."

Once again, Nat didn't reply.

*In a second, Dad is going to say he's made a huge mistake. He's
going to reach out to Fox and tell him he's changed his mind.*

But both remained silent, cocooned inside their own worlds. Back at the cottage, Nat spurned his dad's offer of a late-night hot chocolate on the porch and headed straight for his room. He lay on his mattress, going over and over everything that had happened that night in microscopic detail. He pictured the beautifully lofted pass from Danny that had set him up for the wonder goal; he felt the surge of joy he'd experienced as the ball smashed into the net; he recalled the words of the Rangers manager.

"Just like Pelé, just like Best, just like Maradona—your lad has natural, raw talent."

This was no teen soccer magazine fantasy. This was the real deal. Ian Fox had asked him, Nat Levy, to join Hatton Rangers!

There was only one possible course of action.

He would just have to make his dad change his mind.

But the big question was: How?

22

Stand-off

Dave was in the kitchen making tea when Nat came down the following morning. Before he could say anything, Dave started spouting furiously.

"I feel angrier now than I did last night," he snarled. "Fox was totally out of order!"

"You heard what he said," Nat replied, feeling determined to challenge his dad. "The club will be finished. That's why he made the offer. He thinks I might be able to help stop that from happening."

"Come on, Nat!" Dave snorted. "You're thirteen, for goodness' sake! Fox admitted he's a desperate man. Desperate men have a tendency to lose the plot!"

"But you haven't thought about it properly," countered Nat. "We might be able to make it work."

"No," his dad shot back firmly. "You can join the Academy, but there's no way you're getting involved with Fox's ridiculous idea. Anyway, I want you to carry on shifting junk out of the living room."

Nat was completely taken aback; the change of subject was so sudden.

"You can't just sweep this away, Dad," he said tersely. "You can't pretend last night didn't happen!"

"It did happen, Nat, but it shouldn't have. You're an

impressionable, soccer-loving kid. Only just bar mitzvahed! Fox should have kept his mouth shut."

"But this is the most amazing thing that's ever happened to me!" cried Nat. "I know it's crazy, but I can do it—I know I can."

"No," his dad replied, putting his coffee cup down on the sink and fixing his son with a hard stare. "You can't do it. In three years things will be different."

Nat felt desperation rising in him. "Please, Dad. Can't we work something out? I can go to school as well as joining Rangers. I could manage them both."

"It's not just about school, Nat," Dave replied. "The whole thing could completely destroy our lives."

"But, Dad…"

"No, Nat. I want you to leave it." Dave's tone was firm and final.

Nat did help his father with the living room, but his spirits were crushed.

The two of them ate lunch on the back porch as Nat mulled over his options. They ate the meal in silence, broken only once by Dave asking if Nat wanted a drink.

Nat took a couple of hours off after lunch to practice his shooting and continue thinking things over. He struck the ball, hard and cleanly, into the circles on the oak tree, controlling it on his chest, his shoulders and his head, before smacking it back again. He was extra tough on himself; if the ball didn't hit the absolute center of the circle he was aiming for, he made himself start again. And as he played, he felt a tide of anger sweeping through his body. He couldn't just let this thing go without a proper fight.

By suppertime Nat and Dave were both tired and they devoured their pizzas.

"I've been thinking about the Rangers thing all day," Nat announced when the meal was over.

Dave looked at him wearily.

"Please, Dad; just listen to me for a minute."

"There's no point," replied his dad firmly. "I've come back to England to try and be a responsible parent to you. Saying yes to Fox would be an act of gross irresponsibility. I know it's your dream to play for Rangers, but this is the wrong offer at the wrong time. The pressure's just gotten to the man; he's spouting nonsense."

"But…"

"No," said Dave. "I've made my decision. I can't cancel what Ian Fox said last night, but you've got to try and blot it out of your mind. You're still in shock; we both are. I really don't want us to have a *broigus* about this. Go and get a good night's sleep and I'm sure you'll feel differently in the morning."

Conflict Zone

Nat did feel different in the morning. But not in the way his dad would have liked. The new day brought a cold clarity to his brain.

This is a once-in-a-lifetime opportunity. I CAN'T turn it down!

He tried talking about it at breakfast and lunch, but his father refused to be drawn. Through the afternoon, as Nat lugged garbage bags to the dumpster, anger and frustration rose within him and he began to plot a new line of attack.

He launched his offensive at 5:18 p.m. They were in Lowerbury. His dad had just bought some wires and tools in the town's Hands On Hardware store. He'd caught wind of a drugstore refit in Kellerton—the town next to Lowerbury—and he was determined to be ready to start work on it immediately. If they wanted him, of course.

Nat waited until they'd loaded the stuff into the Mondeo's trunk, got in and closed the doors. Dave stuck the key in the ignition and was about to fire it up when Nat brought up the subject on both their minds.

"I know you don't want to talk about Fox and Rangers anymore, but I need to."

"I can't see the point in talking about it," Dave replied. "It will only upset you."

"Don't you think I'm upset already?" snapped Nat. "You know how much I want to become a professional soccer player. This could be my big break, my only break. What if I don't get another chance?"

"You'll get another chance," Dave replied. "You'll have clubs lining up for you on your sixteenth birthday."

"Can you guarantee that?" Nat demanded.

"Of course I can't guarantee it, but I'm pretty confident about it. Look, Nat, please can we drop this? I've made my decision."

"I'm sick of you making decisions for me!" Nat shouted.

A woman loading an electric drill into the adjacent car looked at them suspiciously.

Nat lowered his voice.

"Do you think I wanted to leave home when Mum died?" he hissed bitterly. "I was six years old! If it had been up to me, do you really think I would have left England?"

"Well … I…"

"NO!" Nat snarled. "You don't know because you never asked me. Well, for your information, I didn't want to go. However devastated I was about Mum, I liked my school and the other kids there. It was a stable place for me. But you pulled me out and took me abroad. I was never given a choice."

Dave tried to butt in again, but Nat hadn't finished.

"Did you ever consider for one second how I felt?"

"Of course I did!" his dad replied hoarsely. "I mean, I tried to." His cheeks were red. His face was pained.

"Well, think about how I feel now!" seethed Nat. "Fox's offer is like … like my destiny. I can't turn it down."

"You *have* to," Dave hit back. "I told you, it's the wrong offer at the wrong time and…"

"BUT THAT'S THE WHOLE POINT!" cried Nat, banging his fist on the dashboard. "The 'right' offer sometimes comes at the 'wrong' time. If I turn this down and I don't get another chance, I'll hate you for the rest of my life."

Dave shook his head fiercely. "No, Nat, you'll thank me…"

"I will NOT thank you!" Nat screamed.

His temper was flowing furiously now. His eyes were orbs of fire leaping across the car in his dad's direction. His heart was pumping violently.

"What is it, Dad?" growled Nat. "Why won't you let me do it? No one knows us. It's not like anyone's going to find us out."

"That's only part of it. There are so many other things to consider."

"This isn't about me and Ian Fox, is it?" said Nat.

"What do you mean?" Dave frowned.

"You're stopping me because your family stopped you going to that Chelsea tryout, aren't you? You're taking that out on me!"

Half of Nat instantly regretted saying this, but the other half was too angry to care.

"DON'T BE RIDICULOUS!" his dad thundered. "I didn't go for the Chelsea tryout because my family was broke. Bubbe and Zaida didn't stop me from going. I made the decision myself."

"Well, I bet you resented them, didn't you? You must have. You could have turned pro but instead you wound up as a carpenter."

"It was my decision," repeated Dave.

"Well, let me make mine!"

"Please," Dave beseeched him. "I was older than you are now. You've got to listen to me…"

But Nat could see he was getting nowhere. "You're screwing up the best chance I'll ever get!" he yelled, pushing open the passenger door and crashing out of the car.

"Wait!" his dad called, stepping out of the car too, but Nat was already halfway across the parking lot. He side-stepped a man pushing an overloaded shopping cart and ran out onto the street. As his feet pounded the pavement, tears snaked down his cheeks.

He dipped into a small alley and caught his breath. He waited until he'd seen the Mondeo speed past on the road before he came out and considered his next move.

24

Cutting Ties

After the bust-up with his dad, Nat was shaking with rage.

I should get away from this dump, he told himself, *away from Lowerbury, away from the cottage, maybe away from England. It doesn't feel like home at all.*

But he had almost no money with him, no clothes, and no idea where to go.

He hung out in Lowerbury for a while, then bought a soccer magazine and slipped into the Lighter Bite for a Coke and a sorrow-drowning chocolate muffin. He thought about the situation from every angle but kept arriving at the same place. If his dad wouldn't agree to it, there was absolutely no chance he'd be able to accept Fox's offer. If he went to Fox by himself, Dave would go straight to one of the papers and blow the whole thing open. Why wouldn't his dad just go along with it—even for a tryout period? It was so unfair!

By the time he returned to the cottage, it was already dark. He heard his father pottering around in the kitchen, but went straight up to his room and slammed the door. He lay on his mattress and tried to cheer himself up by visualizing the most spectacular goal he'd scored during his time in Brazil. It had been during an evening match on Copa Cabana beach.

He'd met a group of kids of all ages, who were taking on a bunch of Brazilian students—all in their early twenties. Despite the informal setting (with water bottles as goals) both sides took the match very seriously.

The game was only five minutes old when a stringbean-thin boy called Roberto collected the ball on what was roughly the halfway line. One of the students harried him, but Roberto shielded the ball tightly and looked up for options. He spied Nat about twenty yards away from the opposition's goal. Roberto tucked the front of his right sneaker under the ball and lifted it toward Nat.

The second the ball left the ground, Nat knew what he was going to do. He took a quick step backward and as the ball descended to a point just in front of him, he launched his body upwards and smacked an audacious bicycle kick. As his back hit the sand, the ball sped through the air. He spun around and saw the goalie dive for it. But he couldn't reach it and it smashed into the goal.

"*Bom de bola*—he's a great player," he heard several people gasp.

Nat felt power and pride in his chest. It felt amazing to score a goal the Brazilian way.

Dave's gentle knocking on his door interrupted Nat's memories of his Rio golden goal.

"Do you want anything to eat?" he asked softly.

"Leave me alone!" Nat snapped back.

Nat heard his dad's footsteps retreating.

On Sunday Nat refused to talk to his father or even

acknowledge his existence. If Dave wasn't going to change his mind, then Nat was going to cut him out of his life. He'd save up enough money and then head off, away from this horrible cottage and horrible life.

While his dad scraped at walls and lugged garbage bags of junk, Nat lay on his mattress, his head pounding, his spirits fully deflated. Dave knocked on his door at one o'clock to ask if he wanted some lunch. Nat didn't even reply. Instead, he grabbed some food later on when his dad was sitting out the front.

Later, when Dave played some Beatles tunes on his harmonica, Nat angrily covered his head with a pillow. He didn't like listening to his dad's musical efforts at the best of times; today he couldn't bear to hear one note.

At 2:30 p.m. Dave called out that he was driving into Kellerton to meet someone about the drugstore job. Did Nat need anything?

Yeah, thought Nat bitterly, *a new life*.

When his dad had gone, he went downstairs, grabbed the radio and returned to bed. It was Rangers vs. Aston Villa—a home game, so surely a chance of snatching at least a point? But Rangers were awful. Their acute nerves clearly got the better of them and they were 2–0 down by half-time, one goal coming from a penalty after a clumsy challenge by Dean Jobson, the other from a free kick, where the goalie, Chris Webb, was unsighted.

In the second half the team played a bit better, especially Robbie Clarke, who was unlucky not to get a penalty when he was brought down in the Villa box. But the ref waved play on and Nat knew that it was going to be another of those afternoons when nothing goes right and you leave the field without any points. When would the players start realizing they were facing relegation and up their game? It was pathetic.

He didn't see his dad again until after six o'clock. They met on the stairs. Dave looked exhausted and agitated. He attempted a conversation, but Nat glided straight past him.

Serves him right; he's just messed up my life—he should feel some of my despair.

They ate supper in shifts.

Dave carried on working well into the evening. Nat sat on the back porch and wished he had a different father.

On his way to bed, Nat glanced into the kitchen. Dave was pacing around the room, with a furrowed brow.

He's stressed? Tough luck. It's a million times worse for me.

Nat flopped down onto his mattress and scrunched up his eyes. How long could he keep this non-communication thing with his dad going?

The answer was simple—forever, if need be.

25

An Unexpected Call

Nat sat on the flat patch of grass in the back field and let the rays of the sun warm his face.

It was 12:35—Monday afternoon.

Dave hadn't been around when Nat got up. He thought he'd heard him leave in the early hours, but what did he care? It was probably to do with the drugstore refit. Dave was more interested in that stupid job than in his son's fractured life.

When a car horn sounded from the front of the cottage Nat ignored it. If anyone wanted to find him they could come out here. He certainly wasn't going to them, even if it was something important connected to the gas or electricity.

But the car horn rang out again, and then again.

Who the heck is it?

Nat thumped his fist onto the ground, dragged himself up, and stomped back toward the cottage. He cut down the side path and emerged out at the front.

There on the drive was the rusty Ford Mondeo, with his dad at the wheel.

Nat stood rooted to the spot and scowled at the dream-destroyer.

"Get in!" shouted Dave.

Nat rolled his eyes to the heavens. "If taking me on a

87

crummy day trip is your idea of compensating for turning down Rangers, you can forget it!" he shouted. "I'm not going to be bought off with a movie and ice cream!"

"I said get in!"

Still Nat didn't move.

Dave waved his right arm frantically in the air. "We've got to move quickly!" he yelled. "COME ON!"

The urgency in his dad's voice made Nat take a few cautious steps forward.

"What's going on?" he demanded.

"I'll tell you on the way."

"Tell me now!"

"No, we're in a hurry."

"A hurry to where?"

"I said I'd tell you in the car, just get in."

Nat hesitated.

Dave's face didn't suggest a day trip. It implied something far bigger. Nat stood his ground for a few more seconds and then hesitantly climbed into the passenger seat.

"This had better be good," he said, frowning, echoing all of the cynical detectives who graced the taut thrillers he devoured.

His dad nodded seriously. "Stick your seatbelt on," he commanded.

Nat was still unsure what to do, but he reached for the belt and clipped himself in.

As soon as he did, Dave slammed his foot down on the gas and the car lunged forward onto the driveway.

26

A Step Up

The Mondeo reached the end of the driveway and Dave pulled out onto the Lowerbury road.

"Now can you tell me what's going on?" demanded Nat.

You've got two minutes, then I'm out of here.

"I was so livid with Ian Fox after Thursday night," his dad began. "I wanted to throttle him for making you that offer."

Nat shifted in his seat.

"I so badly want you to settle down here," his dad went on, "the cottage, school, join a shul, everything."

One minute, thirty seconds—what kind of stunt is he trying to pull?

"But after the fight we had, I made myself start thinking, really thinking, about what you'd said. All that stuff about leaving England without consulting you, dragging you around the world, you always doing what I asked of you. It was an awful lot to expect. To be honest, you've always been awesome."

One minute. Where is this going?

"I mean, as you said, you were only six when Mum died and we set off on our travels. When I was six, the longest journey I'd ever been on was to watch Tottenham Hotspur."

Nat brushed a crumb off his T-shirt.

Thirty seconds.

"So I started asking myself, what if you were right? What if this was your one and only chance in the game and I blew it for you?"

Nat felt a tiny tremor of hope in his chest.

Hang on; let's hear this out.

"What if you never got another opportunity?"

"That's what I've been trying to tell you!" shouted Nat.

"And then, when you said I was envious of you because I missed the Chelsea tryout—that really cut me up."

Nat lowered his eyes. That had been a low blow.

"But, you know what?" said Dave, suddenly dropping his voice, "You're right. There's a part of me—a part I've buried very, very deep—that *is* angry and bitter about not going to that tryout. No one forced me to miss it, it was my own decision, but I was under a lot of pressure—my family was cracking up financially. Over the years I've often wondered how things might have turned out if I'd shown up that day at Chelsea."

Nat gulped.

"Could my own bitterness be making me stop you? Was that the real reason I was saying no?"

Nat stared at his dad, not quite believing what he was hearing. But still, it didn't mean anything. These could be just words—a way of softening Nat up.

"I realized I needed to see everything with fresh eyes," Dave continued. "My rage had completely overwhelmed me. So I began to test Fox's proposal from multiple perspectives. Was there any way I could allow this to happen and ensure it didn't destroy you, destroy us?"

The pupils of Nat's eyes were widening as he looked at his father's anguished expression.

"I struggled with it for hours. I couldn't get to sleep last night, so at about 3 a.m. I made a call."

Every muscle in Nat's body tensed.

"I phoned Ian Fox. He asked me to go straight over to his house."

Nat felt he was about to lose his breath.

The rest of my life could rest on the next few seconds.

"Yes, Fox's plan is illegal and underhand; it's cheating, there's no other word for it. But you said I would ruin your life if I stopped this thing happening and I don't think I could live with that. You were right—even though I am intrinsically bound up with you, it's your life. I know the project is littered with obstacles, but there are certain opportunities in life that you only get once."

Nat's body was shaking with anticipation.

"You mean … you mean … you've changed your mind?" Nat whispered—frightened to hear the response in case he'd gotten it completely wrong.

His dad thought about this for a few seconds. "I suppose I have." He nodded. "Yes, Nat, I've changed my mind."

27

On the Way

"Oh my God!" bellowed Nat, flinging his arms around his dad's neck. "Thank you! Thank you! THANK YOU!"

Dave's hand slipped on the steering wheel, forcing him to swerve and narrowly avoid a grassy bank at the side of the road.

"Careful!" Dave laughed, pulling Nat's arms off him while steadying the car. "We need to get you there alive."

"Where?" Nat's heart was pounding.

"The Ivy Stadium."

"No!"

"Yes," said his dad, "but before you get too carried away, there are certain conditions I ironed out with Fox in the early hours and they're non-negotiable."

"What conditions?" Nat heard himself ask, his voice uneven with excitement.

"All of the conditions are going to be included in a contract that we're going to sign with Fox. The first and most important one is that I will have the right to pull you out of there without any notice, if and when I choose, and Ian Fox will not stand in my way—whatever the situation. I'm your father, your protector, and your legal guardian. You're thirteen. I have to have that safeguard and maintain some element of control. If I think the arrangement is harming you in any way, then it's over and that's final. Do you understand that?"

Nat nodded.

"Of course, you can also pull the plug without any warning," added his dad, "but if Fox wants to end it, he'll have to meet with both of us and give us a minimum of two weeks' notice."

"What are the other conditions?" demanded Nat breathlessly.

"Number two—you'll have to study in some shape or form. Having talked things over with Fox, I can see that mixing school and Rangers won't be possible."

Yes!

"So when the season's over in mid-May, he's agreed to provide a tutor at home."

"Cool," Nat agreed.

"Condition three is about the temptations that may become available, as you'll be mixing with lots of young men, some still in their late teenage years. You are NEVER to smoke, drink, or take drugs. If you do, you'll be out immediately—even if it's just a beer. I insist on zero tolerance in this."

Nat nodded. He'd had a few furtive beers on their travels, but he could easily live without alcohol. As for smoking, he'd tried a cigarette in Germany and it had made him feel sick. Drugs held no appeal for him.

"And number four: you must always let me—or Ian Fox if it's applicable—know where you are and how long you're going to be there."

"Fine," replied Nat. "Is that it?"

"For the time being, yes, but conditions can be added if and when necessary. Remember one thing, Nat—this is an extremely risky business; if we're exposed, Fox, Evans, and I could go to prison."

A cloud darkened Nat's face. He hadn't thought of that.

"I just hope," added his dad, "that I don't end up regretting this."

"You won't regret it," said Nat, taking a deep breath and firmly squeezing his dad's arm.

"We'll be there in twenty minutes," said Dave.

Nat lay back in his seat and closed his eyes. It was totally and utterly incredible.

My all-time number-one dream is about to come true!
I'm joining Hatton Rangers!

28

Sign on the Line

Half an hour later, Nat and Dave were sitting in Ian Fox's office at the Ivy Stadium. It was not nearly as grand as the splendor of the boardroom last Thursday night. Was it really only four days ago that Fox had made his offer?

The office was square, with pin boards on three walls, each covered in notes, diagrams, letters, and photos—both soccer- and family-related. There were several snaps of Fox's two teenage sons, one of whom was at the West Ham Academy.

After the initial pleasantries and Fox's declarations of unbridled delight that Dave had come around to the idea, the Rangers manager turned to business.

"Right, Nat," he began. "From this moment onward you are sixteen years old to the outside world. Your new date of birth is exactly the same as your real one, but it took place three years earlier."

Nat felt a knot of anxiety tighten in his stomach.

Oh my God! This is really happening.

"Fine," Nat replied, mentally trying it out for size.

Question: How old are you, son?
Nat: I'm sixteen.
Question: Really?
Nat: Sure, I just had my sixteenth birthday.

"And your name, from now on, is Nat Dixon."

Nat nodded thoughtfully. Dixon. It had an OK feel to it.

"What about people recognizing me?" asked Nat. "I mean, I haven't got any pen pals or anything, but there are kids all over the place who may remember me."

"I'm sure that getting rid of that mountain of hair will do the trick," Fox replied. "If we need to take any other measures, we'll work them out together."

Nat drew in a deep breath. *A haircut is OK, but I draw the line at plastic surgery. Mind you, it* is *Rangers.*

"Your dad has explained the four conditions to you, hasn't he? Do you accept them?"

"Totally." Nat nodded.

"Excellent." Fox smiled. "Your starting salary will be ninety pounds per week. That's the standard payment for our sixteen-year-old trainees. Next year, when you hit your 'seventeenth' birthday, you'll earn the right to sign professional terms with us, if you're good enough."

Nat tried to look calm as he took in all of these details.

Ninety pounds a week! Sixteen-year-old trainees!

Professional terms!

Fox picked up a red file from his desk. "I phoned Stan Evans at about seven o'clock this morning, after your dad showed up and told me he was willing to give this project a try. I asked Stan to concoct a back-story for you. We've decided to say that Stan spotted you playing street soccer on one of his scouting trips to America. He was very impressed by what he saw and when he discovered you weren't affiliated to any club he set up a meeting with you and your father. He further tested out your skills in a public park and that was enough evidence of your abilities.

"He's deliberately left out any of the finer details of your story since we want to keep the story as simple as possible. It's all here in this file. I suggest you learn the contents off by heart, because you'll be needing them."

"What about signing me, the transfer window, that kind of thing?" asked Nat.

"According to the file, we spotted you last September and signed you before the January transfer window closed. However, due to complications with your paperwork, we've only just got the go-ahead to use you."

"But I wasn't registered during the transfer window. There'll be no record of me," pointed out Nat.

"That's where having a very good contact in the department that deals with that kind of thing comes in handy. And he owes me a big favor. He'll know nothing about your age, but he will backdate your clearance. Don't worry—it'll all be taken care of."

"What happens if someone asks me questions about my past that I can't answer?" enquired Nat.

"Just say you don't want to talk about it," replied Fox. "That will hold them off for a while. Then go straight to Stan and discuss it with him. He's the man with your history—he'll supply you with whatever answers you need."

Nat took the folder and quickly flicked through it. Inside there was a map of the east coast of America and two pages of neatly typed information about his new identity.

Fox then opened one of his desk drawers and pulled out a single sheet of cream paper, covered in type.

"This is the contract your dad mentioned," he explained. "Obviously we can't get lawyers involved, but I think it's pretty comprehensive."

Fox pulled a pen out of his jacket and, with a quick flourish, signed and dated the document. He then passed the contract and pen to Dave.

Dave took a deep breath, signed his name, and handed the contract to Nat.

Nat held the piece of paper between thumb and forefinger. The four clauses were set out in bold type. By signing this he would become a brand-new person. It was terrifying, but also wildly exhilarating.

Tension crackled in the room as if the three of them had just realized the enormity of what they were doing.

Nat lowered the pen. Nat Levy was strictly past tense.

Nat *Dixon*, he wrote.

"Welcome to Rangers." Fox beamed, gripping Nat's hand. "I'm delighted you're joining us. Whatever happens, I'll make sure you're well looked after. And don't worry, I'm not expecting you to save the club single-handedly. I'm not even expecting you to play for the first team—we'll just see what happens. But I do want you to flourish here, so Stan Evans and I will do anything we can to help you settle in."

"Thanks, Mr. Fox," Nat replied.

"Forget the Mr. Fox." The manager smiled. "From now on, you'll call me boss—just like everyone else."

"Right ... boss." Nat nodded.

"Excellent," Fox said, smiling. "I want you in for training tomorrow morning at 10 a.m. The other players will already be here. That way you can meet them all in one go."

Nat shivered with excitement. He was going to be meeting the Hatton Rangers first-team squad; not cardboard cut-outs, not magazine photos, not figures in promotional ads—the real, flesh-and-blood players.

"Make sure you're on time," warned Fox with a serious look. "I'm very strict on punctuality."

Nat met the gaze of the Hatton Rangers manager. 'Yes, boss,' he replied.

29

The Waiting Game

After the meeting with Fox, Nat and Dave went into Lowerbury to buy some hair clippers. Back at the cottage it took his dad twenty minutes to shave off all of Nat's hair. Dave handed him a mirror. The result was astounding. Gone were his long locks, replaced by a very close-cropped head. Ian Fox had been right: it was a brand-new face. Nat didn't recognize himself, so it was unlikely that anyone else would.

In the afternoon they finished clearing the living room. Nat kept glancing at his dad and waiting for him to say he'd changed his mind again, but it didn't happen. The rest of Monday passed in a complete haze. Nat's body buzzed with excitement.

I'll be training with the Wildman and Adilson and the rest of the first-team squad. I'm good, but am I anywhere good enough to fit in? Will I be hundreds of miles out of my depth?

During supper, Dave tried to soothe Nat's frayed nerves. "You're going to be fine, buddy, I'm telling you. I know it's easy to say, but you've just got to try and relax. Evans saw in five minutes on that blacktop court that you're a special player. And you were awesome in the second half of the tryout match. Fox and Evans both saw that performance."

"But what if I clam up and can't even kick the ball?" demanded Nat anxiously. "I'll look like a *klutz*."

"That won't happen," his dad replied. "You'll just play your normal game. Fox and Evans wouldn't have you there unless you were good enough to be there. They'll be there at training to support you."

"I know." Nat nodded. "But it still feels totally overwhelming."

"Of course it does," said his dad sympathetically, "but you'll handle it, just like you handled the tryout match. You didn't go to pieces then."

"True," conceded Nat, "but that wasn't against players of international caliber, was it?"

"It's going to be OK," said Dave. "I'll drive you there and be waiting for you when you come out. You won't be alone."

He stood up and ruffled Nat's stubbled head. "I'm so proud of you, buddy." He grinned. "It's really, really amazing."

Soon after, Dave checked if Nat was OK and announced he was going to bed.

"Don't stay up late fretting," said Dave. "And if you're freaking out during the night, just wake me, yeah?"

"Sure," replied Nat.

But he felt restless, so he walked down to the gas station on Lowerbury road to get a bar of chocolate. The place was about to close and the owner switched off the lights the second he'd sold Nat the chocolate. Nat sat on a bench on the forecourt, eating his late-night snack. The guy from the gas station shouted good night as he headed off in his car.

If only he knew what I'm going to be doing tomorrow!

As Nat tried to visualize tomorrow's training session for the zillionth time, he suddenly found himself thinking about Mum. He would have loved to see her reaction to all of this. Would she have approved? Would the clandestine nature of the deal appeal to her creative side? Or would she have slammed her foot down in the name of protecting her only child? He placed thoughts of Mum to one side and refocused on the coming challenge.

Tomorrow is the day I've been waiting for my whole life. Please, please, please don't let me blow it.

Meet and Greet

As Nat began his walk back to the cottage and the prospect of a fitful night's sleep, Tanner was striding down a road in Totteridge, north London, known as "Soccer Row." Each of the sprawling houses nestled behind high iron railings, with large security alarm units sticking out from the buildings. He stopped when he arrived at Number 47.

He took a quick look both ways down the street. There was no one else around. He pressed the intercom buzzer.

"Yes?" demanded a very familiar voice.

"It's Tanner."

There was a long pause. "What are you doing here?"

"I have a business proposition to discuss."

"What kind of proposition?"

"The kind of proposition that's best not discussed over an intercom."

There was another pause and then a low humming noise sounded as the gates slowly parted.

Tanner slipped between them and hurried over to the house's front door. It was pulled open and a hand beckoned Tanner inside. He went in quickly and a second later, the door was shut, the gates were closing and Tanner was obscured from the outside world.

For Real

Just before 10 a.m. on Tuesday morning, Nat and Dave arrived outside a building that made up a facility called Shelton Park—the Hatton Rangers training ground, situated five miles west of the Ivy Stadium.

To access Shelton Park you took a very narrow turn off the Shelton Road, at the end of which was a high gate. A metal entry pad stood at the side of the track with a number code box. A sign on the gate stated "PLAYERS WILL NOT STOP FOR AUTOGRAPHS." In reality this wasn't the case, as the Rangers fans that waited for hours to catch a glimpse of their heroes knew. But today there were no fans in sight.

Dave wound down the Mondeo window and tapped in the code Stan Evans had given him. The gate swung open and Dave drove through. Nat had seen Shelton Park on TV several times but the pictures hadn't done the place justice. It was huge. There were two full-size training fields in addition to three smaller ones. An enormous steel building was set back from the fields.

My name is Nat Dixon. I'm sixteen years old.

Dave pulled up on the gravel of the car park and he and Nat gazed at the cars already parked there. They were all flashy—not another Mondeo in sight: Porsches, Ferraris,

BMWs. Premier League salaries had certainly sorted this bunch out for wheels.

"Remember," said Dave, putting his arm around Nat's shoulder. "Don't be a show-off, just be yourself. That's the guy that Fox and Evans want to see."

Nat nodded, took a very deep breath and blew out his cheeks. "Wish me luck," he said as he opened the passenger door.

"I wish you all the *mazel* in the world!" said his dad, and with that Nat got out, closed the passenger door behind him and started across the gravel toward the steel building and a sign pointing him to reception.

He walked inside and gazed at the air-conditioned interior. To the left was a water cooler and a long black leather sofa. To the right was another identical sofa and several orchids in glass pots. Straight ahead was a wide oak desk, behind which sat a smartly dressed woman with a Rangers pin on the collar of her jacket. Nat walked toward her.

"You must be Nat Dixon." She smiled as he reached her desk. "Mr. Evans told me to expect you."

Nat was relieved that this wasn't some crazy dream after all, but was terrified of what he was about to undertake. "As you're new here, could you please sign the visitors' book?" she said. "It's just a formality. After today you'll receive player clearance and you won't need to sign in again."

"Thanks," replied Nat, scrawling his name with a shaking hand.

Nat Dixon.

He was just about to ask where to go next, when he spied Stan Evans approaching from a door to the right of the desk.

"Excellent timing, Nat!" The Rangers assistant manager beamed. "I take it Kelly has gone through the formalities."

"He's all signed in and cleared." Kelly smiled.

Evans shook Nat's hand and led him through the door. They walked down a long corridor past several offices, turned left, walked down another corridor and then down a short flight of steps. At the bottom of these was a large black door.

As Evans reached for the door handle, Nat's body clattered like a frantic piece of machinery ripped loose from its bearings. He remembered being nervous before getting called up to the Torah for his bar mitzvah, but those butterflies were kids' stuff compared to what his stomach was doing now.

My name is Nat Dixon. I'm sixteen years old.

But Nat didn't get any more time to think, because Evans opened the door and ushered him inside. As his feet carried him forward, the full force of the moment hit Nat in the solar plexus.

About twenty feet in front of him stood Ian Fox. He was standing next to a whiteboard covered in tactical diagrams. A black marker pen dangled from his hand. The entire Hatton Rangers first-team squad, all wearing fresh training jerseys, were sitting on a horseshoe of benches facing the manager. Eight large ceiling lights gave the space a bright glow. The room smelled of mud, leather cleats, and shower gel.

"Right, lads," announced Fox, beckoning Nat forward, "I'd like you to meet Nat Dixon—the lad I mentioned to you at the start of this session."

All eyes swiveled to take in Nat.

Nat scanned the room. There was club captain Neil "the Wildman" Duffy, and that was the brilliant Brazilian winger, Adilson. Further down was giant goalkeeper Chris Webb. In the right-hand corner was right-back Kelvin Bartlett. He was sitting next to Italian central-midfielder Paolo Corragio. In the left-hand corner sat the brilliant young center-back, Emi Adeyo.

Nat had seen these figures hundreds of times on the small screen, but up close they looked completely different. For a start, they were far bigger. And although they looked lean on TV, now he was among them he could see that most of them didn't possess even the tiniest ounce of fat on their muscular frames.

He took a couple of tentative steps toward the circle of light overhanging Fox. Evans moved with him—a minder, someone to grab if he keeled over from the seismic shock of coming face-to-face with the legends gazing back at him.

"As I explained, Nat's a center-forward," said Fox. "Stan spotted him on a scouting trip to the US. Luckily we signed him before the January transfer window, but we've had to wait a while to sort out his paperwork."

Part of Nat wanted to scream, *I'm a fraud! I'm a liar! I'm thirteen!*

Evans picked up the thread. "Nat's English but he hasn't lived in the UK for seven years, so we want you all to make him feel extra welcome."

There were a few "hellos" and nods in Nat's direction. Nat nodded back, feeling exposed and full of trepidation.

What if one of them starts grilling me about my past? He'd memorized everything in Evans's red file, but it was only pretty basic stuff.

"Take a seat beside the Wildman," Fox said, indicating a space on one of the benches.

The Wildman shifted along at the end of one bench and gave Nat a wide grin. Nat walked over on trembling legs to take his place. The captain reached out for a handshake. Nat responded and his fingers were crushed by the Wildman's powerful grip.

"Welcome to Rangers," the Wildman said. "We could do with some new blood around here."

Nat's heart was beating so fast that he felt sure it was going at a medically unrecognizable speed. He had to force his legs not to jiggle frantically.

"Right," said Fox, drawing the attention of his players back toward him. "I know you all feel dejected, but as I've told you a thousand times, we can stay up. I'm convinced we will stay up. But the fight back must begin on Saturday, against Chelsea. I know we're playing at their place, and I know they're on fire at the minute. They can't win the league, but they're playing for third place, so they're going to give us a serious testing. But for us the stakes are far higher. Lose, and we'll slide a bit further toward the exit ramp of the Premier League."

There were nods of assent around the room.

"The boss is right," cut in the Wildman. "I don't know about you guys, but I'm not too keen on playing in a lower division next season."

Several players murmured in agreement.

"Yeah, the money's rubbish," said striker Steve Townsend sourly.

The Wildman gave Townsend a fierce look. Townsend looked away sullenly.

"OK, then," Fox concluded. "Let's get going."

The players rose and started moving toward the door at the right end of the locker room.

Nat stood up too, but Fox stopped him. "How does it feel to be here?' the manager asked quietly, with a glint in his eyes.

"It's … it's amazing," Nat managed to reply, still feeling the aftershocks of being in the same room as the squad. "It's unbelievable."

"Good." Fox smiled. "Now I know you're pretty fit, Nat, but training will probably be a bit of a shock to your system. I work the players hard. OK?"

"Totally, boss."

"Good lad." Fox winked. "Now get that stuff on"—the manager pointed to some fresh jerseys on a bench—"and show everyone what you can do."

32

Out There

Pulling on a brand-new Rangers training jersey was amazing enough. But emerging from the changing-room door and trotting toward one of the full-size fields where the semi-circle of players was standing was truly awesome. The field had been beautifully maintained; a huge expanse of green lay before him.

He stepped onto the grass gingerly—afraid it might rise up in protest at the appearance of a thirteen-year-old. But the grass stayed silent and Nat jogged forward to join the others. Despite the fact that he felt like a tiny kid among men, he was relieved that he'd spent much of the last year building up his muscles and in particular his upper-body strength.

Fox was starting the training session and demanded immediate attention. To begin with, he took everyone through some stretches. Nat's cleats rested snugly on the freshly cut grass and he made himself blot out his surroundings and just try to concentrate on Fox's voice.

Just do what he tells you and don't fall over.

During the stretches, Nat stood near center-back Emi Adeyo, who grinned at him and mouthed the word "boring." This gesture took a tiny slice off Nat's nerves, as did a wink from Kelvin Bartlett.

Next, Fox ordered everyone to run around the field three times. Nat ran beside the two regular central-midfielders, Paolo Corragio and Dean Jobson. Nat was a big fan of them both, although he knew they'd crossed swords before over whose responsibility it was to defend and whose it was to attack. Some critics in the media said the two of them couldn't be accommodated on the same team.

After circling the field, there was a series of cross-field runs, some forward, some backward, and some sideways. Nat eased himself into them, careful not to overdo it.

Next the players split into pairs and worked on short passing. Fox teamed Nat up with Pierre Sacrois, the gangly but very fast French right-midfielder. Sacrois took his soccer very seriously and Nat worked hard trying to keep up with the Frenchman's high standards. Short passes were then swapped for headers, with Nat and Sacrois taking turns to lob balls at each other to head back. Sacrois didn't speak once.

After that came sprinting, and then dribbling around long lines of cones. Nat was a tiny bit off the pace of the fastest runners.

Keep it together, man, you're doing OK.

Fox pushed the players hard, tinkering and fine-tuning the activities, making them repeat tasks if he felt anyone was coasting.

"Chelsea are very good at keeping possession," the manager reminded them. "They're specialists at frustrating opponents and wearing them down. We need to break things up and get on the ball; play them at their own game—keep possession and frustrate them."

The next half-hour was spent in groups. The defenders went off with Fox to work on tackles and intercepts. The midfielders focused on tracking back and tackling.

Nat joined the other strikers—Steve Townsend, Robbie Clarke and first-choice reserve striker Dennis Jensen. They would be taking shots at first-team goalkeeper Chris Webb and reserve goalie Graham Dalston.

As Nat followed the others over to the goal at the far end of the field, he felt a twinge of panic setting in. So far, he'd been able to remain pretty anonymous in this training session—he'd worked hard and tried to remain inconspicuous. Now that he was with this small group he felt much more vulnerable.

I could so easily be exposed here. What if I'm total rubbish compared to them?

Chris Webb shouted that he and Dalston would take turns between the sticks. Townsend went first and scored. Clarke hit the post. Jensen's low and powerful strike was saved by Webb.

Then it was Nat's turn. Dalston rolled a ball out. Nat breathed in deeply.

This was it. His first ever shot as a Rangers player. He struck it as hard as he could. Unfortunately he hit it too hard and skied it well over the bar.

It doesn't matter. It was only your first one.

He waited nervously for his turn to come around again. Townsend and Clarke both scored. Jensen hit the post.

Nat's second shot went wide. His third was weak and easily held by Dalston.

He was beginning to feel slightly desperate and felt anxiety lashing against his chest. He needed to up his game—immediately.

33

Hitting the Net

Luckily, Nat's fourth shot was strong and on target. Chris Webb saved it, but he had to dive. Jensen nodded approvingly at Nat, while Townsend looked on with a sneer. Nat struck his fifth effort toward the top left corner of the goal. Dalston leaped toward it, but its pace outdid him and it crashed into the back of the net.

Nat had to stop himself from punching the air and pulling his top over his head. He'd got his first goal against a Premier League goalie! OK, it was only in training, and it wasn't against the first-team keeper, but Dalston was a good shot-stopper—it had to count for something. He imagined massed banks of supporters yelling his name and leaping around in celebration.

His next three shots were saved, but he scored with his ninth, a curler that spun beneath Webb's outstretched body. He'd now beaten both goalies—a reason to feel a tiny bit of pride.

Nat was relieved when Fox called everyone back together. Although he'd managed to hold his own in the shooting practice, the individual nature of the task had stretched his nerves badly.

I'll get used to it—I just need some time.

Fox then announced they were going to play eight vs.

eight on one of the smaller fields, for two halves of twenty minutes each.

Nat was on a team that included Robbie Clarke, Andy Young, Pierre Sacrois, and Kelvin Bartlett. He was to partner Clarke in attack, and they'd be facing the Wildman and Emi Adeyo—the rocks at the heart of the other team's defense.

From the kick-off, Nat instantly saw that however low morale was at the club, the majority of players badly wanted to be on the winning side—even in this training match.

He was involved a couple of minutes after the kick-off, when Sacrois stroked the ball to him. He trapped it and passed it straight back. It was simple, but he'd done it: his first match pass in training. He saw more of the ball a few minutes later, when it broke from a corner and landed at his feet. He picked out Clarke with a long raking pass. He then had a chance to shoot just before half-time, but Emi Adeyo stretched out his leg and pulled the ball away.

In the second half, Nat made some good passes— nothing flashy, but accurate—and toward the end of the game he had another shooting opportunity. Sacrois slipped him a pass just outside the penalty area. Nat didn't even think about it. He just unleashed a hard, curling ball. It arced and lifted off the turf as it sped goalward. Chris Webb had to stretch to push it over the bar.

"You cheeky monkey!" The Wildman laughed, slapping Nat on the back so hard he felt like his ribs were about to salsa-dance their way out of his ribcage.

Five minutes later, the game and the training session were over. Nat allowed himself a private smile: training session one completed, without any disasters. The players trooped back into the locker room, while Fox and Evans disappeared somewhere else. Nat fell into step with Adilson. It was still completely mind-blowing to be out here on the field, but his uncertainty and fear had dropped a tiny measure.

"Not bad for your first go." The Brazilian grinned. "They must have taught you well in the US."

Nat smiled but said nothing.

Back in the locker room, Paolo Corragio came over to say that Nat had done well in training and the Wildman gave him another hearty slap on the back. They were small gestures but they meant a lot to Nat.

He watched the other players depositing their shirts, shorts and socks in a large steel box and followed suit.

What a joy. Someone else to wash your jersey!

There was a huge stack of freshly laundered green and white towels resting on a shelf, and Nat took one.

The showers were covered in expensive green and white tiles. The faucet and shower fittings were ornate and silver. There was soap, shower gel, and moisturizing cream, neatly laid out on each tiled shower shelf. Nat let the luxurious water cascade over him. He knew he had a very, very long way to go to prove himself, but he'd done OK out there. With luck, no one would be thinking, "Get that lousy kid out of here!"

Adilson was in the shower next door, singing a song about a guy who can't get his girl. He sang half in Portuguese, half in English. He was a hopeless crooner—completely out of tune—which made Nat laugh.

After changing, Nat was just packing up his bag, when Emi Adeyo and Kelvin Bartlett wandered over.

"Wanna come for something to eat?" asked Bartlett.

Adeyo was a very strong and agile player—often tipped as a future Rangers captain. He was six foot three, with cropped black hair and intense, dark-brown eyes. He was nineteen, but had already played ten games for the Ivory Coast. Bartlett was twenty, and the regular right-back in the England under-twenty-one team. He was small, muscular, and shaven-headed, with a thunderous shot—a bit in the mold of Brazilian legend Roberto Carlos.

"Sure," Nat replied. "I'll be with you in a minute."

34

Opening Up

Twenty minutes later, Nat, Emi Adeyo, and Kelvin Bartlett walked into the café on the top floor of Shelton Park. It had a great view over the soccer fields and the countryside beyond. The other customers were a couple of groundsmen and three plasterers who were working on some new office space within the facility.

"So how did you find training?" asked Emi, as they sat down at a table in the far corner.

"It was pretty intense," Nat replied, "but I guess I expected that."

"What do you make of the lads?" asked Kelvin. Nat hung back. He'd have to be very careful here.

"Adilson's a good laugh"—Emi smiled—"apart from his singing. He should be entered for the Worst Vocal on Earth competition."

Nat laughed. "Yeah, I heard him in the shower."

"We mostly hang out with the younger players," said Kelvin. "Adilson especially. Andy Young's also a good laugh."

"Most of the older guys are OK," added Emi, "especially the Wildman, but they're all a bit, you know, middle-aged."

"Paolo Corragio is a good guy," said Kelvin, "but he and Dean Jobson hate each other."

"What do you think of the boss?" inquired Emi.

"He seems OK," Nat ventured.

"Yeah." Kelvin nodded. "He is OK, but he has two personalities. He's really tough if you do something he doesn't like; he might not talk to you for weeks. But then he can go all friendly again."

As Emi and Kelvin started arguing over which of them had gotten the biggest scolding from Fox, Nat realized that for the first time that day he was starting to relax a little. He was just wondering where you ordered your food, when a big, bustling woman with frizzy light-brown hair came over to their table carrying a large tray. On it were three plates piled high with grilled fish, salad, and steamed broccoli.

"This is Amalia." Emi grinned. "Amalia is the queen of this place. Her food is fantastic and her service second to none!"

Amalia laughed as she put the plates down in front of them. Nat stared at the food hungrily—he'd hardly eaten anything all day.

"Someone told me there was a new player in today." She beamed, wiping her hand on her apron and shaking Nat's.

"This is Nat Dixon," said Kelvin. "Stan Evans spotted him in the States. He's a striker."

Amalia clapped her hands. "At last!" she declared. "I've been telling Mr. Fox for months that he needs someone new up front. Townsend and Clarke haven't exactly been banging in the goals, have they?"

Nat felt himself blushing.

"Give him a chance to settle in," cautioned Emi. "There are only four games left."

"I know, I know," said Amalia wistfully, "but we just can't go down. It would be a disaster!"

Amalia left and they dug into their food. The conversation moved on from training and Rangers to their favorite films and then their musical tastes. Kelvin had just bought an incredibly expensive new cell phone with a state-of-the-art music facility, and he lovingly displayed it for them.

To Nat's surprise, when they stood up to leave, there was no check, and no payment was made.

"Club account," Emi explained, noticing Nat's puzzled expression. "Who said there was no such thing as a free lunch?"

They stepped outside and hung around for a few minutes. Kelvin fiddled with his new phone while Nat and Emi looked on in amusement. Despite the sense of relief Nat felt at hanging out with Emi and Kelvin, he reminded himself that he wasn't their equal. He was only thirteen. He was untried at any formal level, let alone the goldfish bowl known as the Premier League. Emi and Kelvin were experienced professional players; both had represented their countries. Nat existed on a different planet from them.

"Hey," said Kelvin, snapping Nat out of his thoughts. "We're going back to my place. I've got this excellent new computer game, *Shark Death*. Come along, man. I'll give you a lift in my Merc."

"You are such a show-off, Bartlett!" Emi laughed.

Nat stole a glance at the low-slung silver Mercedes in the garage. It stood just a few spaces away from the Mondeo, in which his dad was reading a newspaper; it was slightly embarrassing being picked up by your dad after training with the Hatton Rangers first-team squad.

"Thanks," replied Nat, "but I've only been back a little while and I've still got loads of settling-in stuff to do."

"Cool." Kelvin nodded. "Another time?"

"Definitely," replied Nat.

Emi and Kelvin both slapped Nat on the back before heading off toward Kelvin's wheels. Nat realized that he had been so surprised that Emi and Kelvin had asked him to join them for lunch that he'd left his bag in the locker room. It would only take a few minutes to go back and get it. He'd run in, grab it, make sure no one was around to spot him climbing into the Mondeo, and then give his dad the blow-by-blow account he was waiting for.

35

A Warning

Nat's bag was exactly where he'd left it on one of the benches. He snatched it up, exited the locker room and started walking down the hall. Reaching the steps at the end, he was about to start his ascent when he suddenly felt a strong hand gripping his left shoulder. The hand pushed him roughly through an unmarked gray door. As he stumbled inside, the hand released him.

It belonged to Steve Townsend.

Nat's stare moved from Townsend's contemptuous face to his surroundings. They were in a small, square, whitewashed room with a mesh of wires and pipes sprouting out of the far wall. Townsend stood inches away from Nat's face. His breath smelled of chewing gum and iron. Townsend's expression was menacing, his eyes dark pools of fury.

"Now listen well," Townsend hissed, "because I'm not going to repeat this."

Nat stared back uncertainly.

"This is the way things work at this club," snarled Townsend. "I'm the center-forward. It's my place and mine only."

Surely Townsend isn't threatened by me? I've only just gotten here.

"I saw that shot you tried in training this morning," Townsend went on. "Very nice, very impressive."

He does feel threatened.

"It's disgusting to see a snotty-nosed kid like you kissing up to the manager on your first day at the club."

Nat stared back at Townsend, whose face was twisted with anger.

"You're treading on dangerous territory." Townsend wagged his finger in Nat's face. "I suggest you back off immediately."

"Back off what?" Nat asked.

Townsend pressed his face closer. "Don't play innocent. You think you're hot stuff—I can see it. In your dreams, you think you can take my place."

Nat held Townsend's stare.

"I mean it, Dixon," Townsend continued. "I don't want you anywhere near the center-forward position. Fox and old-man Evans have tried to draft in other strikers, but they've all failed."

Nat was tempted to bring up Townsend's poor scoring record in the last couple of months, but decided it wouldn't be great timing.

"There are at least another couple of seasons in me and no one's going to stand in my way," said Townsend. "So I'm warning you. Try any heroics and you'll end up hurt. Keep it simple and you'll be fine. Do you get what I'm saying?"

Nat nodded very slowly. He watched in silence as the Rangers forward glared at him for another few seconds. Then Townsend spat on the floor—missing Nat's feet by the narrowest of margins—before storming out and slamming the door behind him.

36

A Grilling

The second they were past the front security gate, questions exploded from Dave's mouth.

"How did Fox introduce you? Did anyone say hello? What's the Wildman like? How did training start? Could you keep up with the rest? Was there a game at the end? What did Fox say about the Chelsea match?"

Nat responded to each question, trying to give as much detail as possible. By the time they'd made it back to the cottage, he'd dealt with all of them.

But his dad wasn't finished. "What about your size?" he asked. "Did you feel out-muscled?"

"No," replied Nat, "but the challenges weren't that tough. In a real game they'd all go in much harder."

They were now approaching the cottage's door. "Was Fox pleased with you?"

"I think so."

"What did you do when the session finished?"

"I went to the café with Kelvin Bartlett and Emi Adeyo. It's run by this mad Rangers fan called Amalia. I think she's Italian."

"So no bagels, then." Dave laughed.

"No." Nat smiled. "But the food was pretty good."

Dave's eyes widened. "Incredible," he murmured. "You hung out with Bartlett and Adeyo on your first day!"

"They're really normal," replied Nat. "And they gave me the low-down on the club."

"I'm finding it hard to believe any of this is really happening," said his dad, "so it must be crazy for you."

"It is." Nat nodded. "But it's better than going to school!"

Dave frowned. "Just because you're not going to school doesn't mean you'll never go!"

"OK, OK; it was a joke."

Dave grinned. "I have a little surprise for you," he said, ushering Nat toward the kitchen. Nat walked inside and stopped when he saw the two items in the corner. One was a fridge, the other was a stove.

"I got them in Lowerbury," Dave told him. "They were a bargain. Secondhand, but in almost perfect condition. So tonight I'm going to cook us our first proper meal!"

"Excellent!" Nat grinned. "About time too," he whispered under his breath.

So while Nat went upstairs and read a soccer magazine, his dad clanked around in the kitchen, whistling to himself. After half an hour of reading, Nat put the magazine down and closed his eyes. The next thing he knew, his dad was waking him up, telling him it was 7 p.m. and time for supper. Nat was astonished.

He'd slept for three hours in the middle of the day— that must be what training with a professional club did to you. Dave had cooked spaghetti with meat sauce—Nat's all-time favorite meal. They ate in the kitchen, sitting at the table and using real cutlery.

"What was Steve Townsend like?" asked his dad, twisting some coils of spaghetti on his fork.

Nat felt a tight knot in his stomach. Should he tell his dad what had happened with Townsend? He took a sip of his drink. "I didn't have much to do with him," he replied.

"I've heard he's a bit of a moaner," said Dave, "but maybe he saves that for newspaper reporters! How about Paolo Corragio? That lad has got a bit of a temper on him."

"He seems OK," replied Nat, enjoying the flavors of the dish.

Nat polished off his food. He took his and Dave's dishes over to the sink, washed and then dried them. "I'm going to get an early night," he announced. "Training in the morning."

Training in the morning; how quickly life could change!

37

Staking a Claim

Unlike the day before, when he'd met up with total (but instantly recognizable) strangers, when Nat stepped into the Shelton Park locker room on Wednesday morning, he felt a tiny sense that he wasn't completely out of place.

He'd told his dad that he didn't need to drop him off today. It hadn't taken long to convince him. After all, here was a thirteen-year-old boy who had traveled miles by himself on trains and buses, in countries as far apart as India and Switzerland. Dave could hardly worry about a couple of sedate English bus rides.

So Nat took the bus to Lowerbury and then another one that stopped a hundred yards from Shelton Park on the Shelton Road.

"Are we glad to see you!" Emi beamed as Nat dumped his bag on one of the changing-room benches.

Emi then turned around to check who was around. "We didn't want to pressure you on your first day, but we need you to replace old whiny Townsend. We need to farm him off to another club—if anyone will take him!"

Nat laughed and got changed.

"All right?" said the Wildman, coming over to Nat and shaking his hand.

"Uh, yeah," replied Nat.

"Good." The Wildman grinned. "It's great to have you with us. Maybe you can inject a bit of a spark to the end of our season. We could do with some uplift!"

On the field, Evans and Fox got involved immediately, with stretches, runs, passing, and shooting. Evans then asked the forwards, including Nat, to come with him. He began chucking balls their way, at all heights and speeds, expecting them to catch the balls on the volley and whack them into the empty net. Nat concentrated hard and his strike rate was pretty good. Steve Townsend glared at him a couple of times but that was it.

Then Evans got them running, slow and fast, accelerating and decelerating. Nat coped well with the exercises and felt a fraction less nervous than yesterday.

In the eight-a-side game at the end, Nat was pushed up in a two-man attack with Dennis Jensen. He acquitted himself well, passing with accuracy, having a couple of decent shots saved by Chris Webb and making an excellent tackle on Dean Jobson. Evans gave him a nod halfway through the game, which Nat took to mean he was doing OK.

At the end of the match and the session, Evans took him to one side. "I'd like to see you shooting a bit more tomorrow," he said. "You were unselfish today; you passed a couple of times to Dennis Jensen when you could have had a go. Being selfish is a key component of the striker's make-up. Sometimes you just have to go for it, OK?"

Nat nodded.

"I also want you to build up your upper-body strength," Evans continued, "get a bit more meat on you to deal with defenders. If you're too lightweight they can just flick you out of the way."

Nat knew this made sense.

After training, Kelvin had to go and do a photo shoot for a men's fashion magazine and Emi was off to see a cousin who was in London for a couple of days. This was fine with Nat. He had work to do. He'd thought he was at the top of his fitness curve, but training with the Rangers squad showed him he had a huge amount further to go. So he spent an hour and a half in the gym, doing free weights to build up his upper-body strength and cycling to work on his thigh and calf muscles.

He caught his two buses home and when he got in, his dad was sitting at the kitchen table, holding the phone in one hand while scribbling on a piece of paper with the other. He looked up when Nat walked in and indicated he'd be finished shortly.

"That was someone about the Kellerton drugstore refit," said Dave, a few minutes later.

"Any luck?" asked Nat.

"Possibly," replied his dad. "It would be a good couple of weeks' work. I'll be really upset if it doesn't come through."

"If it doesn't you'll find something else," replied Nat. "You always do."

"I need to find something soon. There are bills to pay, plus the mortgage on this place."

"I'm earning now," said Nat. "I know it's only ninety quid a week but it'll help pay for some of that stuff."

His dad stood up. "Thanks, Nat; you're a good kid, but there's no way I could accept money from my thirteen-year-old son, even if he does have a contract with a Premier League team."

"That's crazy," replied Nat. "You've paid for me for all these years, it's fine that I put some money in now."

"No," said Dave sternly. "It's up to me to sort this place out. I'm the one who dragged you back to England, so I'll be the one who sorts it all out. Your money is for you, to spend on what you like."

"But, Dad…"

"No, Nat," insisted his dad, "it's not up for discussion. I'll get something soon and it'll all be OK. And anyway, far more importantly, how was your second day?"

Nat filled his dad in, but his response was far shorter than yesterday's. He thought quite a bit about his dad's refusal to accept any of his money. Why did his pride prevent him from seeking a bit of financial help from his son? Dave could be totally pig-headed once he'd made a decision. But then Nat remembered something. Weren't those almost the exact words that his dad sometimes used to describe him?

Screen Time

On Thursday after training, Emi came up to Nat in the locker room.

"Why don't you come over to my place?" he offered. "Kelvin's coming and I've got some excellent new computer games. *Dawn Stake Out* hasn't been released in Europe yet but I got a copy from my friend in the States. It's awesome!"

And so Nat found himself sitting in the living room of a small townhouse half a mile away from the Ivy Stadium, playing computer games with two international soccer stars.

Nat had always been under the impression that all soccer stars lived in gated mansions in the commuter belt, with high privet hedges to keep out the prying eyes of the general public. But Emi had lived in a rented room for the year and a half he'd been at the club.

"I love it," he told Nat. "Mrs. Felgate cooks all of my meals and washes all of my clothes! What could be better?"

The three of them were cheering each other on and yelling at the army of Wolf Warriors, whose job it was to stop them from entering the Emerald Castle.

"You're good!" Kelvin laughed, giving Nat a friendly thump on the shoulder.

Nat grinned his thanks. How many hours had he spent playing computer games on his travels? Thousands. Not that he was a gaming addict or anything, it was just that he'd always managed to find people who had game consoles and were willing to let him play.

It was dark by the time they finally wrapped up, leaving a virtual trail of devastation in their virtual wake, all of their eyes stinging from overexposure to the pumping screen visuals.

Dave was out when Nat got back to the cottage, so he fixed himself some scrambled eggs and sat on the back porch listening to a soccer phone-in show on the radio. After talking about the upcoming European Champions League Final—Barcelona vs. AC Milan—the host switched to the relegation battle at the foot of the Premier League. To Nat's despair, almost every caller included Hatton Rangers in their "three sure to go down."

Nat shouted at the radio, "Don't write us off yet! We've still got four games to play!"

But his intervention went unheeded. It was the general consensus that Rangers were going to drop.

The atmosphere during Friday's training session was different from the previous three days. With most clubs, the nearer a game loomed, the more fired up the players became, but with Rangers that wasn't the case. Games meant real points—real points they'd been losing all season. The Chelsea match represented an opportunity and a curse. Tying or (if miracles happened) winning would be supreme, but losing… Unfortunately, because of their dips in form and their doses of bad luck this season, losing was in the forefront of everyone's mind. You could almost smell the fear on the training fields at Shelton Park.

As Fox and Evans shouted instructions at them, quite a few of the players were jittery. So much rested on these last four games. Many of them had huge mortgages on houses they'd bought when they'd gained promotion to the Premier League; a reckless move to many, but the amounts of money that had started sloshing around were large enough to turn anyone's head.

In every player's contract there was a "Relegation Clause," which stipulated the massive downsizing of salaries if the club dropped out of the top tier, but until now no one had taken much notice. Now, suddenly, the small print felt very threatening.

Fox worked with the forwards toward the end of the session, and he worked them hard. They went through loads of different scenarios in the Chelsea box and he kept on flagging up the weak spots of the two Chelsea central defenders.

"Matt Holmes is too right-footed. Turn him on his left foot and he won't reach you. Carl Nash drifts a long way up the field—much further than his manager can stand. All it takes is one good pass to split their defense. They're good, but they're not that good and they've conceded plenty of goals this season."

They worked for ages on crosses and headers, pulling in the Wildman and Emi to jump with them. "And another thing," declared Fox. "Just remember that Holmes is a bit of a nasty piece of work. How many times have you seen him leading with his elbows? Take advantage of that. I'm not saying to go sprawling in the box at the first opportunity. What I mean is, if he catches you—if he really connects with you—then go down. Hit the deck, hold your face. It doesn't have to be a West End performance, but the ref might take heed. Holmes has given away three penalties like that this season. Another one would be most welcome."

When training was over, everyone trooped back to the locker room. There was little conversation and none of the usual banter. These players knew the season's endgame was about to unfold and they were all too aware of how much was at stake.

Nat took ages in the shower and when he came out most of the players had gone. Chris Webb was just lacing up his black shoes and Adilson was shaving and singing another Portuguese song. Stan Evans popped his head around the door. When he spied Nat, he came in. He was carrying something.

"I've got you a couple of tickets for tomorrow's Chelsea game," Evans explained. "For you and your dad. I tried to get you ones right behind the team, but it was impossible. They're still pretty good seats, though."

"Thanks, Stan … I mean, Mr. Evans," said Nat gratefully, gazing down at the tickets.

"My pleasure." Stan winked. "You can repay me by scoring for us at the first opportunity!"

Nat tucked the tickets into his jacket pocket. He'd only been at three training sessions and already he was getting plum seats for the next Rangers game. Not bad for a boy who should have been starting school soon.

He walked out and cut through the players' parking lot. Maybe one day he'd drive a fancy car like them, or maybe not. If Rangers got relegated, he was sure some of them would have to trade in their Ferraris for Fiats. For the umpteenth time he recalled the speech Ian Fox had made to him and Dad on his tryout night.

If we get relegated, Rangers will cease to exist.

As a lifelong Rangers fan, that was a devastating prospect, but with Nat's involvement now as a player, it took on a far greater meaning. Fox had given Nat his chance at Rangers. If Fox were ousted, would another manager be prepared to take him on? What if they started looking too deeply into his past and discovered the truth? If they did and he was exposed, he might never get a chance to play professionally. After coming this far in such a small space of time this possibility was more than bad news; it was absolutely devastating.

39

An Appointment at the Bridge

The smell of fried onions wafting out of burger vans permeated the street as Nat and Dave walked toward the looming skyline presence known as Stamford Bridge, the home of Chelsea soccer club. It was 2:45 in the afternoon. There'd been a long delay on the Tube so they'd cut it a bit fine for a three o'clock kick-off, but they were here now.

A large man in a long black leather coat—a ticket scalper—cast his gray eyes up and down the street. "Anyone got tickets to buy or sell?" he called out, loud enough for passers-by to hear, but quiet enough so the police standing twenty feet away didn't.

The stands of three program sellers took up the next section of pavement. Nat and his dad stopped to buy one. It was packed with Chelsea news and features but gave over four pages to "Today's Opposition." Nat scanned the pictures of the Rangers squad, looking at them now in a new light. These players were no longer two-dimensional cut-out-and-keep heroes to him: they were real people.

They reached the turnstiles and Dave opened his shoulder bag for a steward to inspect.

"It's only apples and a couple of bottles of Coke," Dave explained.

"No problem." The steward smiled. "Enjoy the game."

"Cheers," said Dave, as first he and then Nat scanned their tickets against the electronic entry port and were buzzed in through the very narrow turnstiles.

The place was a hive of activity. Some people were making straight for their seats; some were watching highlights of recent Chelsea games on wall-mounted TVs; others were lining up to buy overpriced snacks and soft drinks.

They checked their ticket numbers and headed up a flight of stone steps. As they emerged into the warm afternoon breeze, Nat felt the pulsating thrill he experienced every time he saw a real soccer field. The expanse of green was vast and full of possibilities. On their travels, he and his dad had seen Ajax play in the Netherlands, Maccabi Tel Aviv in Israel, the Japanese national team in Tokyo, and Boca Juniors in Brazil. Each game had been an incredible experience, particularly the last. Brazilians certainly knew how to party!

Their seats were in the upper tier, just past the halfway line, facing the tunnel. The players had already been out for their pre-match warm-up, and kick-off was only a few minutes away.

"Good afternoon and welcome to Stamford Bridge!" boomed the stadium announcer over the speaker system. "In a minute we're going to meet both teams, so here are today's line-ups."

"For Rangers, in goal, number one, Chris Webb!"

A small round of cheers sounded from the Rangers supporters, but these were quickly drowned out by the hisses and boos from the home fans.

"Number two, Kelvin Bartlett!"

Kelvin's name got the same treatment, as did all the other Rangers players. Then it was time to announce the Chelsea team.

"In goal for the Blues, Welsh international, and club number one, Roy Farrow!"

The Chelsea fans went crazy, screaming out Farrow's name, whistling and shouting.

"Number three, our ever-present left-back, Jerome Pattere!"

Huge roars of approval met Pattere's name. On and on, the announcer went through the Chelsea team, each name being greeted by deafening approval. The loudest cheer of all, though, was saved for the legendary Chelsea center-forward, Adusa Kloss, the half-Ghanaian, half-German bulwark, who'd opted to play for the Germans in the international sphere.

"Watch Kloss's running off the ball," said Dave. "We all see those brilliant runs he makes into the penalty area when the ball is fed to him, but when the ball is passed to someone else, he always finds a space just level with the last defender; he's the best I've ever seen at that."

Nat normally treated his dad's advice with the utmost humility, knowing he still had so much to learn. But today, Dave's words grated on him slightly and he made a decision not to track Kloss too closely—even if he did miss out on a trick or two.

And then the teams were marching out of the tunnel into

the bright afternoon sunshine, to the rapturous applause of all in the stadium.

"Come on, Rangers!" shouted Dave, a bit too loud for Nat's liking. This was Stamford Bridge, after all. A couple of seriously tough-looking Chelsea fans shot Dave a sour look. He didn't call out again.

Rangers won the toss and opted to take the kick-off. As the ref blew and the game started, the volume of noise in the stadium rose to an almighty crescendo. And the home fans had something to cheer about before ten minutes were up. In the ninth minute, Robbie Clarke lost the ball just inside Rangers' half. Jerome Pattere whipped it away from him and found Kloss with a long-range pass. Kloss dummied a shot, which left Andy Young sprawling on the turf. Kloss then pounded in a vicious, curling left-foot shot.

Chris Webb's eyeline was blocked by a retreating Dean Jobson, and the ball smashed into the top right corner of his net. The Chelsea fans went crazy. Nat and his dad stared in silence, as the fans of less successful teams do week-in, week-out. However bad your team's luck or performances have been, it's still always a mighty shock to concede a goal so early in a game.

"Going down, going down, going down!" sang the Chelsea fans, some of them sitting directly behind Nat and Dave. Nat gritted his teeth and silently willed Rangers on.

And to his surprise, the team didn't let him down. Chelsea's scoring had lit a fuse beneath the whole Rangers team, and they suddenly upped their game—led by Adilson.

For the next fifteen minutes he seemed to be everywhere, screaming for the ball, beating men and spraying a range of gorgeous passes to waiting teammates.

"Put the ball away!" muttered Nat under his breath.

At twenty-nine minutes, Adilson pounded up the left sideline. He muscled one Chelsea defender away, faked out a second and impudently nutmegged a furious third. He looked up, saw Steve Townsend screaming for the ball at the far post ... and ignored him. Instead, with ferocious spin, he lofted the ball goalward. Roy Farrow in the Chelsea goal pawed at the ball, but it evaded him and sailed into the net.

The Rangers players mobbed Adilson, with the exception of Steve Townsend, who stomped back to the Rangers half, fuming at Adilson's selfishness and ignoring the fact that the Brazilian had actually scored.

Nat and Dave had to use all their willpower to stop themselves from leaping into the air in the midst of their solid-blue surroundings. Such a triumphant display wouldn't go down well in these parts.

It stayed 1–1 until half-time.

After the break, the Chelsea fans poured back inside the stadium, grumbling about their team letting Adilson have that shooting opportunity and about the "luck" of his "unintended" shot. They all seemed convinced that Chelsea would turn it around in the second half. That was the confidence you got through supporting a top team.

Nat and Dave, on the other hand, felt that heady elation they hadn't experienced for months when it came to supporting their team. Instead of losing their heads as they had done all too often this season when they went behind to an early goal, the players had defended solidly and set their attack dog, in the shape of Adilson, on the loose. And it had worked. Drawing 1–1 at half-time at the Bridge wasn't a scoreline to be scoffed at.

Nat thought about what Ian Fox would be saying to the team in the locker room. Would he praise them for the way they hadn't gone under at 1–0, or would he yell at them for giving away yet another early goal? Nat figured the manager would unleash a bit of both.

For the first fifteen minutes of the second half, Rangers kept in the game. The Wildman was outstanding at the back—a colossus in white, company-sponsored cleats. He out-jumped the Chelsea forward line, out-ran them and out-thought them. Adilson continued to menace the home team and broke through for a one-on-one with the keeper, only for Farrow to dive bravely at the Brazilian's feet and claim the ball. But then disaster struck.

On sixty-two minutes, Andy Young leaped up when a Rangers corner came in and headed the ball into his own goal. It was one of those classic situations; if his head had been tilted a little bit to the right, the ball would have gone out for a corner and his teammates would be congratulating him, instead of giving him filthy looks, or, in the case of Steve Townsend, screaming at him.

The Wildman grabbed the ball from the net and kicked it toward the center circle. He ran around the field, shouting at his players, trying to instill a new sense of urgency and purpose in them. It was 2–1—so what? There was plenty of time left to get another equalizer, maybe even go on and win the game.

Rangers attacked with intent. Chelsea found themselves on the ropes and had to defend pretty heroically to keep the ball out of Farrow's goal. Adilson came close with a long-range effort and Steve Townsend missed a sitter, following a cross from Sacrois. Nat watched the time running down on the huge stadium clock and crossed his fingers tightly, hoping against the odds that Rangers would score again.

In the eighty-fifth minute, after Robbie Clarke had hit the crossbar, Farrow booted the ball into the Rangers half. It hit a divot on the ground and bounced strangely, wrong-footing both Jobson and Corragio. The ball ran on to Kloss, who deflected off a challenge from Emi and smacked it home.

Instead of running for the ball to get things started again, Jobson and Corragio squared up to each other. Corragio was screaming something in Italian, while Jobson was howling a string of curses against his teammate. Nat and Dave looked on in stunned silence as the Chelsea fans roared with glee. Then Corragio pushed Jobson in the chest and Jobson staggered backward. Sensing the severity of the encounter, the Wildman rushed in and, with the help of Emi, separated his two warring players.

Nat couldn't hear what the Wildman was saying to his confrontational charges, but he got the gist of it by studying the Rangers captain's face. On the sidelines, Ian Fox was hopping around as if he were walking on hot coals.

"Jobson and Corragio are totally out of line!" hissed Dave furiously.

As the final whistle went and the Rangers team dejectedly stumbled toward the tunnel, Jobson and Corragio returned to what they'd started earlier. Fox stormed over to them and physically separated them, yelling at both of them and dragging them by the elbows, like two naughty toddlers, into the depths of the tunnel.

Like statues, Nat and Dave sat rooted in their seats as all the Chelsea fans surrounding them strode to the exits— delighted with another victory that they'd fully expected and felt entitled to.

"I don't know how Fox is going to pick their spirits up off the floor this time," said Dave glumly. "And as for Corragio and Jobson ... what were they thinking? These guys are paid thousands each week and they end up fighting like two playground kids who haven't discovered the meaning of the word 'share.' It's a disgrace!"

Nat thought about responding to this tirade, but he couldn't summon the energy so remained silent. While he and his dad had held onto tiny strands of hope on the way into the stadium, on the way out, menacing clouds of hopelessness surrounded them. Sunderland had also lost, to Manchester City, but Wigan and Bolton had tied their respective games, which meant they were both now three points clear of Rangers.

Wigan	30 points
Bolton	30 points
Hatton Rangers	27 points
Sunderland	26 points

There were now just three games to go—Tottenham, Liverpool, and Man United. Each one was a tough game, but they had to get something out of all of them if they were to retain even the slightest chance of staying up. It was a huge task, and with the team so despondent—not to mention Corragio and Jobson going for each other's jugulars—it felt like an impossible job.

So it was with very low spirits that Nat and his dad walked away from Stamford Bridge. They continued in silence until the pale yellow lights of the underground station swallowed them up.

40

Dangerous Developments

Nat woke up at 11 a.m. and lay in bed thinking about yesterday's Chelsea game. How on earth were Rangers going to stay up if they carried on playing like that? The only three players who'd had a decent game were Chris Webb, Emi, and Adilson. In fact, if it hadn't been for Webb's heroics, Chelsea could have gotten seven or eight.

Sacrois and Corragio had been shockingly bad, Kelvin had hardly touched the ball, and Steve Townsend and Robbie Clarke had had a terrible time. On the one hand, the strikers' shortcomings could be good, because they might give Nat a chance of a few precious seconds on the field. But on the other hand, Nat was a Rangers supporter and he didn't want useless strikers on the team. He wanted goals, and loads of them.

He traipsed downstairs and found the *Sunday Crest* on the kitchen table. He flicked straight to the sports section and one article immediately caught his eye. It was entitled "Ripping Rangers Apart" and was by their chief soccer reporter, Ray Swinton. Nat scanned the first few paragraphs.

Relegation-threatened Hatton Rangers plunged to even lower depths last night when two of their players staged

an explosive dressing-room row after their on-the-field clash during the side's 3–1 loss to Chelsea at Stamford Bridge. Dean Jobson and Paolo Corragio haven't enjoyed the easiest of relationships this season, but things boiled over after yesterday's dismal performance.

A Rangers insider told the *Sunday Crest*: "This wasn't just some run-of-the-mill post-match spat; this was a full-blown fight. The two of them were really going for it, screaming at each other, attacking each other's playing style, and questioning each other's commitment to the team." Rangers manager Ian Fox had to step in and separate them at the mouth of the tunnel. But the dispute continued away from the gaze of the public and our source disclosed that the post-match atmosphere in the locker room was "complete poison."

The *Sunday Crest* can reveal that both players were kept back after the game by Ian Fox, who gave them a dressing-down. In the words of one observer, he was "absolutely livid." When questioned, a club spokesman said this was an "internal disciplinary matter that will be dealt with away from the glare of the media spotlight and in the appropriate manner."

Nat dropped the paper back on the table and took a deep breath. Rangers staying up in the Premier League? Forget a tall order—this was Empire State Building territory.

Nat remembered the ninety pounds Stan Evans had handed him when they met very briefly after the Chelsea game.

I could do with a new pair of sneakers.

He grabbed his keys and exited the cottage.

He'd been tempted to go to Oxford Street in central London on his search, but he couldn't face the vast crowds. So instead he caught a bus to Lowerbury and the train to Hatton Town station.

Hatton Town center was OK. He'd noticed it had a couple of sports shops so he headed for the first of them—the Sports Cellar. He passed a street seller offering pizza slices, and an unscrupulous-looking guy selling fake designer watches from a suitcase perching on an upturned crate. He went into the Sports Cellar and was pleased to see a vast array of soccer shirts, cleats, and sneakers.

There were the latest Hatton Rangers home and away jerseys as well as those of all the other Premier League teams. After a lot of browsing he spotted a pair of blue-and-white suede sneakers. They were cool, and he tried them on. They felt great as he performed a couple of small jogs and a few jumps. Two minutes later he left the shop, swinging a bag with the sneakers inside. He'd just spent the first money he'd earned and it felt good.

He did a little window-shopping, bought a slice of pizza and a Coke, sat on a bench reading the soccer coverage in the day's paper, and then headed back toward the station, cutting through some of the narrow roads surrounding the Ivy Stadium. He'd just entered one of these roads, when up ahead he saw a familiar figure: Steve Townsend. He seemed to be in the middle of a heated discussion with a tall, wiry, shaven-headed guy wearing a dark-blue pinstripe suit.

Nat's first instinct was to turn back and get as far away from Townsend as possible, but curiosity latched onto him and he crouched down behind a row of cars, and crawled to within earshot of the dispute.

"Are you backing out, then?" demanded Townsend in a threatening tone of voice.

"No," replied the pinstripe guy, "it's going to happen; we just need to get the date right."

"We're in this together," warned Townsend in a threatening voice. "We're going to sort this together, do you get me?"

"A hundred percent," replied the pinstripe guy, "and it will be very soon."

Nat frowned. *It's going to happen. We'll sort this together.* What were they talking about?

He was about to inch a bit further toward them when Townsend suddenly turned and looked straight in Nat's direction.

Nat froze for a second but then quickly started scurrying back down the road behind the shield of cars. He rounded the corner, stood up and ran. His heart was beating wildly and he didn't stop running until he was on the platform of Hatton Town station.

As he waited for the next train, two questions burned in his brain.

What were the two of them talking about? And did Townsend see me?

*

Much later that night, Tanner received a phone call. The number was withheld, so he answered with a curt, "Yes?"

"It's me."

Tanner felt a tiny thrill of satisfaction. It was the player from Soccer Row—the one he'd recently visited.

"I've had a long think about your proposal," said the player.

"And?"

"Count me in."

Tanner felt like a boy whose mom has just allowed him to have a family-sized pack of candy.

"And you're fully clear about all of the terms?"

"Yes," answered the player. "I'd like to go over some of the finer points with you, and I'd like to know a little more about the figures behind it, but other than that, yes, I'm in."

"Excellent," said Tanner, "but there is one other thing."

"Which is?"

"Not a word about this to anyone. Not to your wife or your best friend. Do you understand me?"

"What do you think I am?"

"I don't think you're anything; I just want you to understand the size and seriousness of this project."

"I do."

"Good," replied Tanner. "I'll be in touch soon."

41

Vote of No Confidence?

What should have started as a relaxing public holiday began with a startling interview on the radio. On waking, Nat checked his watch. It was just after noon. He flicked on his bedside radio and was just rubbing the sleep from his eyes when the presenter, John Yale, introduced the next guest: Hatton Rangers chairman Steve Pritchard.

> Yale: So Mr. Pritchard, three games left of the season and your huge investment in Hatton Rangers is looking like a complete waste of money.
>
> Pritchard: Come on, John. There are still three games to play. That's nine possible points. Anything can happen.
>
> Yale: But surely, considering the amount of money you've put into the club, Rangers should be miles out of the relegation zone.
>
> Pritchard: Unfortunately, soccer doesn't work like that.
>
> Yale: It seems to work for Manchester City and Chelsea.
>
> Pritchard: But that's not comparing like with like. Those clubs have far greater match-day revenues and

merchandising income. Yes, I've invested in the club, but not on that kind of scale.

Yale: So maybe we're missing the point here. Perhaps the squad Ian Fox has assembled is simply out of their depth?

Pritchard: I totally disagree with that. Neil Duffy and Chris Webb are incredibly experienced players, and we've got people like Adilson, Adeyo and Bartlett coming through; young players, I concede, but players who are already operating at a top level.

Yale: OK, so let's turn to the manager. Is this dreadful season all down to Ian Fox?

Pritchard: I wouldn't call it a dreadful season. We've won some very tough games and tied some even tougher ones. That doesn't sound dreadful to me.

Yale: Dreadful or not dreadful, do you think Rangers' current status is down to Ian Fox's poor management?

Pritchard: The club has a lot to thank Ian for. Don't forget, he's brought us up from the fourth tier to the first. The club will always be indebted to him for that.

Yale: I accept that, but once again I'd like to know if you think Fox has reached the end of the road at the club? Is it time to bring in some fresh blood?

Pritchard: I wouldn't like to comment on that at this present moment.

Yale: So you're thinking of sacking him?

Pritchard: I don't want to talk about Ian Fox or any of the other people employed by Hatton Rangers. I'd far prefer to discuss next Saturday's Tottenham game. We need to get something out of it.

Nat switched the radio off and sat up. If ever a chairman had failed to give a vote of confidence to the manager, Pritchard just had. In the past, even only a few weeks ago, Pritchard was giving his unequivocal backing to Fox. Today he didn't even want to talk about him. Surely by keeping silent on the matter, he was demonstrating that he'd lost confidence in Fox.

Nat went downstairs, grabbed an apple and went in search of his dad. He found him pulling up weeds and straggly ferns on a section of the back field just in front of the stream. The field was bathed in sunshine and looked like a young child's first attempt at drawing some countryside.

"Need a hand?" asked Nat.

"Definitely," his dad replied, his face red and drenched in sweat.

Nat immediately got to work, grabbing huge fistfuls of the green-brown weeds and stuffing them into one of the black garbage bags Dave had brought out. The plants scratched Nat's lower arms, but he hardly noticed. He was too busy thinking about Steve Pritchard's radio interview and who might be the next Rangers manager, because it had sounded like Pritchard had finally run out of patience with Ian Fox.

Nat worked for a good couple of hours, the sun warming the back of his neck, the sweat pouring off him. His arms felt the strain of so much continuous action. At two o'clock, Dave said he'd get them some lunch and disappeared inside the cottage. When he returned he was carrying a tray laden with two giant cheese sandwiches, two large red apples, and two cans of Coke.

Nat walked toward him and they met under the shade of one of the oak trees. Dave set the tray down and they both flopped onto the ground and took a sandwich each. They sat in silence for a while, listening to the gentle trickle of the stream and some noisy sparrows that were perched on the wooden gate at the side of the cottage.

"What was Mum like?" asked Nat suddenly.

His dad looked at him. "You know what she was like, buddy. I've told you lots about her, haven't I?"

"Yeah, you have, but most of that was facts about her: where she was born, what her family was like, where she worked—that sort of thing. I want to know what she was like when you were sitting next to her in a room."

Dave closed his eyes for a moment and a ripple of pain passed over his face. He opened his eyes. "Well, for a start, she always smelled of jasmine. I don't know if you know what jasmine smells like, but it's a sweet, intoxicating smell—not overpowering, but strong enough to draw you in. It was the soap she used. And she laughed a lot. I tell you, Nat, we had some huge laughs. She had a great sense of humor—at least, she laughed at my jokes. And her laugh was infectious; whenever she cracked up, I started laughing too."

He smiled at the memory. "And she was proud," he continued. "Proud of herself and her achievements, proud of being Jewish, proud of you and all the *nachas* you gave us…"

He smiled again. "Her hair was long and curly, and she washed it every day; she was big on cleanliness. If she'd seen how infrequently I bathed you during those early days on the road, she'd probably have killed me!"

Nat felt a lump in his throat, as he always did when he heard his dad talking about Mum, but this time it wasn't simply a sad lump, there was an element of good in there—a confirmation that she had been real, that she wasn't just some phantom that his mind haunted him with.

"Do you remember her?" asked Dave.

Nat stroked his left cheek while he thought it over. "I think I do. I think I can see her face in my mind's eye, but then sometimes I think my memories are just from your photos of her. But I'm sure I remember her voice. Sometimes when I'm speaking I can almost hear her voice in mine."

"You're so right," replied his dad with a heavy sigh. "In the early days, sometimes it was very difficult for me to hear you talk, you sounded so like her."

"But I was only six," pointed out Nat.

"I know, but that was the thing about her. She had retained so much of that aura of youth that so many of us adults shed on the way. She was a free spirit, a non-conformist. The kind of grown-up who loves going on the rides at the fairground long after the other adults have chickened out."

Nat laughed. He so wanted to share what he was going through with her, but of course that would never be possible. He'd just have to make do on his own, with his dad's support.

42

Suspicions Raised

Training was tough on Tuesday, and Nat's problems centered on his left ankle—which he badly twisted in a challenge on Adilson. After getting changed, he limped out of the locker room and tried to give his dad a call. But reception was poor, so he followed the hall around a bend and up a short flight of steps. Reception was a little better here. He passed through another door and found himself in a room just off the back of the training-ground kitchens. Someone was sitting just around the corner—he could see their legs.

Curious, he walked further forward to see who it was. He instantly wished he hadn't. It was Steve Townsend, sitting on a low sofa, a laptop perched on his knees. He heard Nat and looked up. His face instantly contorted. He stood up, gripping the laptop with his right hand.

"What are you doing here?" he snapped.

"I was just looking for better cell phone reception," answered Nat.

"You think I'm going to believe that?" hissed Steve.

"I don't know what you mean," said Nat, holding up his iPhone to show he was telling the truth.

Townsend edged toward Nat. "I said, tell me why you're here!"

"This is stupid," said Nat, "I'm out of here."

"Not so fast!" snapped Townsend, grabbing Nat by the wrist. "I thought I told you to stay away from the center-forward spot the other day. Not only have you blatantly ignored my advice, now you're stalking me!"

"Stalking you?" replied Nat with a bitter laugh. "Why would I want to stalk you?"

"You tell me!"

"You're out of your mind!" Nat shouted, yanking his wrist out of Townsend's grasp. He started to hurry back across the room.

"I'm warning you!" yelled Townsend, "Stay away from the team and stay away from me, or you'll live to regret it!"

"Yeah, yeah!" said Nat, pushing open the door and exiting the room.

He walked back down the steps and only realized when he was at the bottom that he was shaking.

43

Thick Blue Line

Wednesday, Thursday, and Friday passed in a blur for Nat. Training was intense. Like the previous week, by Friday the tension at Shelton Park had cranked up. With no points garnered from the Chelsea game, the home match against Spurs on the weekend was even more vital than before. Rangers simply couldn't afford to lose.

Ian Fox talked on and on to his players about two of Tottenham's stars, their goalkeeper, Brad Short, and their center-forward, Lee Carshalton.

"We've studied countless examples of Short's performances," said the manager, "and we know he gets flustered by crosses and free kicks—so we'll pack their penalty area. Any deflections off him, shoot when you get a chance—I'm telling you, he's vulnerable. Lee Carshalton, on the other hand, is playing superbly and that's been reflected in his call-up from the under-twenty-ones to the full England team for the friendly match against Croatia. Although he's a bit lanky and gawky, he's amazingly quick and once he's past you, you've lost him. If we want to contain Spurs, he's the guy we need to stop playing."

In spite of the very short time he'd spent with the squad, Nat already felt completely wrapped up with them and was beginning to think more as a player than as a fan.

The previous night, he and his dad had stayed up for ages, sitting on the back porch and talking about the Tottenham game.

"The tickets that Stan Evans gave us for tomorrow are fantastic!" exclaimed Dave. "Before we came back to England, I wasn't sure whether we'd be able to go to any Rangers games and now we're regulars! It's incredible!"

"Let's hope we get a decent result," muttered Nat nervously.

"You will." His dad smiled. "bad luck is like an unpleasant smell: it lingers but always goes away eventually."

*

Knight was sitting with four "investors" in the penthouse of a nearly finished apartment block in London's East End. The apartments had been fashioned out of an old garment warehouse and shared a street with a trendy café, a graphic design company and some independent filmmakers. The penthouse was huge, with tiny spotlights dotting the ceiling and glass double doors leading out onto a sweeping balcony. The first tenants weren't expected for five weeks, so the men had the building to themselves.

"Are you sure he's going to show?" asked one of the four, a thin, angular man, with stubble covering his chin and aviator sunglasses perched on his head.

"He'll be here," replied Knight.

As if on cue, the penthouse door swung open and Tanner strode in with a figure close behind him. Two of the four waiting investors opened their mouths, the third took a sharp breath in and the fourth shook his head in surprise. It wasn't every day that you got to meet a bona fide Premier League star.

"Gentlemen," announced Knight, "you all know Mr. Tanner, and I don't think our guest needs any introduction. His football record speaks for itself, and our plan has been very carefully outlined to him. And I'm pleased to say he has agreed to all of our conditions, isn't that right?"

The player nodded solemnly.

"It's excellent to meet you," said the man with the stubble reverently, "but I'd like to know how easy it's going to be to pull this thing off. I mean, can you give us a hundred percent certainty?"

"Nothing can ever be a hundred percent," replied the player coolly, "but I know how much is riding on it and I'm confident I can pull it off."

Knight nodded his head with satisfaction.

"Will it be possible to convince people at the club that what they see is real?" asked one of the other investors, a man with a scar on his left cheek and very dark brown eyes.

"I know exactly what I'm doing," replied the player. "You deal with the finances, I'll deal with what happens on the field."

"Think of this man's standing at the club," said Knight. "He's a hero to fans and players alike. His name is so far below the radar it won't even register."

The four investors looked at each other and then leaned their heads together for a whispered consultation. Knight gave the player an approving look. The player's face remained expressionless.

While this huddle was going on, Tanner heard a noise on the street below. Most other people would have missed it, but he'd trained himself to detect even the quietest sounds. Silently he stepped over to the other side of the penthouse and glanced out of the window.

In the alley running along the back of the flats was a large police van. Spilling out of its rear doors was a team of police officers, wearing full protective gear and hard hats, and carrying machine guns. The officer in charge was silently directing them inside the building.

Tanner quickly turned away from the window.

"I think we may have a problem," he told the others.

One minute later, the front door of the penthouse was smashed off its hinges with a loud thwack. Officers poured inside, brandishing their guns and yelling, "ARMED POLICE!" They fanned out and swarmed through the flat.

It took fifteen seconds for them to check out every corner of the apartment and call out "AREA SECURED!"

Their tip-off had come from a very reliable source, but on this occasion the bird had flown. Someone had been here, but now the flat was completely empty.

44

The Call-up

Nat snatched at his cell phone and instantly dropped it. Here he was, being woken up by its ring at 8:32 a.m. Who dared to phone him this early? He was tempted to leave his phone on the floor, but scrabbled around for it and finally lifted it to his ear.

"Hello?" he answered groggily.

"It's Ian Fox."

Nat sudden felt awake. He sat up in bed. "Yes, boss?"

"Half an hour ago Robbie Clarke fell down some stairs while carrying one of his kids' computers and smashed his right arm," said Fox. "He's in a lot of pain and has just been whisked off to hospital. He asked one of the ambulance crew to phone me on the journey with an initial analysis, so they did and they're pretty sure he's broken it. Either way, he won't be playing this afternoon, so Dennis Jensen will take his place."

Nat's heartbeat was out of its traps and accelerating fast. Could this possibly be leading where he thought it was?

"Jermaine Clifton can play up front," went on Fox, "but it's obviously not his ideal position. So that leaves an out-and-out striker's place on the subs bench. I'm at the stadium; I want you here by 11 at the latest."

Nat leaped out of bed. "DAD!" he yelled.

At 9:45 a.m., after Nat had run around the cottage like a wild thing, grabbing a shower, munching on the toast that Dave had made him eat and talking endlessly, they drove down the Lowerbury road.

"This is incredible," whispered Dave, half with shock, half with excitement. "I knew Fox rated you highly, but this is something else."

Nat nodded nervously. His stomach was churned up with anxiety and disbelief.

I'm going to be on the subs bench for a Premiership match.

They pulled up outside the Ivy Stadium players' parking garage just after 10:30. The security guard stepped out of his box and looked the Ford Mondeo up and down as if it were an enormous bag of dirt that was threatening to foul up his pristine manor house.

"This is a private parking garage," he said, eyeing the Mondeo's passengers suspiciously. "There's public parking in the Drayton Shopping Center and some pay-and-display spots on Horsley Road."

"Er, this is Nat Dixon, and I'm his father. Nat's a sub for this afternoon's game. Robbie Clarke's injured."

The guard frowned. He was on first-name terms with every Rangers player, including all of the reserves. Were these guys trying to make him look stupid? He peered inside the car at the teenager and shook his head.

Obviously Fox and Evans had forgotten to notify the guy.

"I'm serious," insisted Dave. "Just phone the manager's office, or Stan Evans. They'll vouch for us."

The guard pursed his lips. He was inclined to turn these two away with a harsh word, but something held him back. He knew Ian Fox was a wily operator and he'd sprung several surprises before. So he stepped back into his box and tried Stan Evans's office number. Evans picked it up immediately and, seeing the security guard's name on the phone's digital display, knew exactly what he was calling about.

"They're genuine," said Evans. "I forgot to warn you." And so, ten minutes later, Nat and Dave found themselves sitting in Ian Fox's office once again with the Rangers manager and Stan Evans.

"Excellent to see you both," said Evans, giving Nat a reassuring smile. "Robbie has definitely fractured his arm, although thankfully it's not as bad as we first thought. But he'll be out for six weeks."

Nat and Dave exchanged a glance.

"That means you'll be on the bench today," continued Fox. "It doesn't necessarily mean you'll be there for our other two games—we'll see how you handle the pressure today."

Maybe I'll get a couple of minutes on the field?

"We thought you'd like to see this," said Evans reaching onto the table. He held something up. It was a Hatton Rangers shirt.

Evans turned it around. Nat stared open-mouthed at the back of the shirt.

DIXON

"What do you think?" asked Evans, grinning.

"I ... I ... think ... it's amazing!" enthused Nat.

"And you're going to handle this exactly as we discussed?" asked Dave, looking expectantly at Fox.

"Precisely," replied Fox. "People will obviously wonder who this lad is—a player whose name and squad number aren't even on the back of the program."

"It will look very strange," said Dave.

"We'll make it look normal," insisted Fox. "We just stick to the story, especially when it comes to the press. You know my contact at the Association has got the requisite paperwork in position. All we need to do is remain calm."

Nat's whole body shook with tension. Keeping calm was going to be a serious challenge for him today.

He took the shirt and inspected it.

"OK," said Fox. "The rest of the players will get here between about 12:30 and one o'clock. Stay in here with your dad for a while, Nat. I don't want you going down to the locker room by yourself and getting all worked up before anyone else is there to calm you down. Stan and I have a couple of things to do. We'll be back at 12:30 and then you go down, OK?"

Nat nodded, the nerves popping in his body like fireworks. Fox and Evans departed and for the next hour and a half, Nat covered every inch of ground in the manager's office. He paced and paced, talking at his dad in between bouts of deep thought, trying to psych himself up for the occasion without freaking out too much. Fox was as good as his word and, just after 12:30, he and Evans returned.

"OK," said Fox. "I've just seen a couple of cars in the players' garage. It's time for you to go down."

45

Pre-match Workout

Nat swallowed hard. His dad stood up and hugged him. "Good luck, buddy," he said, smiling. "Mr. Evans has gotten me a ticket right behind the players. I'll be rooting for you all the way."

"Thanks, Dad."

"You've got nothing to worry about," said Fox. "We'll see you down there in a little while."

Nat grabbed his shirt and made for the door.

As he walked down to the locker room he was lost in thought. Everything so far had seemed like a surreal dream, but this was different. This wasn't turning up at training or even a reserve match. This was diving in at the deepest point of the deep end. This was Hatton Rangers and the Premier League.

Andy Young and Jermaine Clifton were already in the locker room when he got there.

"The boss told me Robbie broke his arm and that you're on the subs bench," said Clifton, walking over to shake Nat's hand. "Welcome to the club!"

This was all news to Young. "No offense to you, Nat, but we badly need Robbie at this stage of the season."

Nat's heart lurched, but he nodded at Young. What he said made complete sense. Robbie Clarke was a great player—they'd sorely miss him. Dennis Jensen was good, but not up there with Clarke. As for Nat ... he just hoped that if he did come on, he wouldn't let the team down.

The other players arrived in dribs and drabs and Nat was incredibly relieved when Emi showed up.

"Fantastic news!" shouted Emi, running over to him. "Shame about Robbie, though."

"I know," agreed Nat. "What a terrible time to break your arm."

A bit later, Emi was joined by Kelvin and Adilson and the three of them kept Nat talking, giving him loads of encouragement and attempting to soothe his nerves. And then the Wildman arrived and came straight over. The other three left Nat with the captain.

"How are the nerves?" asked the Wildman, sitting down on the bench next to Nat.

"Shot to pieces," Nat replied.

"I still get nervous before every match."

Nat looked up at the Wildman with a disbelieving look. Surely the Wildman was just saying this to make him feel better?

"I swear it," insisted the captain. "If you're not troubled by nerves, you might as well not show up."

The Wildman's words reassured him ... a bit. "You'll be absolutely fine, Nat. If you do get a game, there'll be ten other players and thirty thousand fans out there, and we'll all be rooting for you. You're not alone, OK?"

Nat nodded. The Wildman always seemed to find the

right words for any given situation. But when the captain moved away, the dread level in Nat's body kept increasing.

At 2:30, the team left the locker room with tracksuits still on and headed straight to the tunnel. Nat's nerves were jangling with anticipation. He was aware of each footstep he took in the dark interior until he emerged into the brightness of the stadium. If seeing the field from the stands hit him in the solar plexus, walking out onto it at ground level was a million times more powerful.

Even though there were only a couple of thousand supporters in the stadium at that time, it still felt incredible to walk out and see them. As he stepped onto the field with the rest of the squad, he shaded his eyes from the sun and jumped in the air several times, stretching his limbs. Stan Evans distributed some balls and Nat concentrated on exchanging passes with Emi and Dennis Jensen. Nat spotted several people pointing at him with questioning looks.

If only they knew the truth!

"Have a crack!" shouted Chris Webb, rolling a ball out to Nat.

Webb easily caught his first shot. His second missed the right post. But his third went in. He felt a jolt of encouragement in his chest.

I've put a ball away at the Shipper End—another first to be cherished forever!

His fourth went in as well, but Webb held his fifth. Following this, Evans called all of the players together and they did some short runs, jogging and then speeding up, and repeated the process several times. Every minute more and more people were spilling into the ground. Next Nat exchanged several long, low passes with Adilson and then it was time to head back down into the tunnel. Once inside the locker room again, the eleven selected players changed out of their tracksuits; the five subs, including Nat, kept theirs on.

"Come on!" shouted the Wildman, his booming voice carrying around the whole place, "We're going to do this today!"

Most of the other players shouted back, their faces beginning to light up with resolve and passion. At 2:45, Ian Fox came in. He motioned for quiet and suddenly every player was focused on him.

"I want you to remember what we've talked about in training all week," he began. "Brad Short is a weakness and if we don't exploit that, we may as well go home now. Think of those goals we've studied. I want the Wildman and Emi up for every corner."

"Yes, boss." They both nodded in response.

I'm not just an onlooker now, I'm part of this!

"What we mustn't do is commit too many players for set pieces. So when Emi and the Wildman do go up, I want you—Paolo and Dean—covering for them."

The two midfielders nodded.

"The other thing to watch is their counter-attacking—that's their strength. As I've told you, you particularly need to watch Lee Carshalton. He's lightning-quick and he'll try and skin us. But he is stoppable and often overstretches himself. The main thing is not to panic—no flying challenges that hand them a penalty!"

The players' gazes were locked onto the manager's animated face.

"We owe it to the fans to do well today," said Fox, his voice dropping several decibels, which had the effect of making every player lean in toward him. "We're going to fight for our place in the Premiership and stay right here. I need every one of you to run yourselves into the ground. We HAVE to walk away from this game with something."

Fox paused and there was a tense silence for a few moments.

"OK, lads," growled the manager, his voice rising again. "IT'S OUR STADIUM, THEY'RE OUR FANS. LET'S MAKE IT OUR GAME!"

46

This Is It

A minute later, it was time to go out—and this time, for real. Fox ushered his team into the tunnel. The Tottenham players were already there, lined up and ready to go. The Rangers eleven took their places beside them. Nat stood with both sets of subs, behind the teams. He recognized all of the Tottenham players from TV: there was the goalie, Brad Short, right behind him was the wily Spanish central-midfielder, Fernandez. And of course the number-one threat—Lee Carshalton.

Some Tottenham players were juggling with balls, others were doing stretches. Kelvin gave the Tottenham left-back, Keith Devonshire, a friendly slap on the arm; they knew each other from their time in the England under-twenty-ones. There were several other handshakes between old friends.

"OK, everyone," called out the referee at the front of the lines. "Let's go!"

As the players and subs emerged from the tunnel, they were met with a deafening roar. Nat thought the stadium walls might collapse, so great was the noise. It crackled with the energy of hope and anticipation. The whole place was awash with flags, scarves, and giant Rangers-style hands. It was an ocean of green and white.

Not wishing to be outdone, the Tottenham fans gave a rousing chorus of "You're going down!" which was met by a hearty "Who are ya?" from the home crowd.

As the two teams strode onto the field, Nat walked with the subs toward the technical area, his body alive with electricity. As he gazed up at the vast banks of supporters he heard someone shouting, "Who on earth is that?"

It jolted him, but he reminded himself that there was going to be an awful lot of that today. To everyone in the stadium, particularly the Rangers fans, he might as well be a Martian. He took his place in the technical area, with the reserve keeper, Graham Dalston, on one side and the second-string center-half, Dave Swan, on the other. The stadium announcer started to read out the names of the Tottenham players, each of which was met with a cheer from the Spurs fans and huge boos from the home crowd. Then it was time for the Rangers team.

The Rangers fans went crazy at each name, with the Wildman receiving the highest volume. Then it came to the substitutes' names, which got smaller cheers. And last but not least the announcer called out, "and a first appearance in the first-team squad, for number thirty-three, Nat Dixon!"

Nat's name was met with bewilderment. Thousands of programs were flipped onto their back covers in search of this mystery player, but to no avail.

Up in the press box, Ray Swinton of the *Sunday Crest* scratched his head. The media hadn't been handed the

Rangers team in advance today. This was highly unusual. Was it because this Nat Dixon had been added at the last minute? Swinton knew everything there was to know about Rangers—he followed the reserves and the youth teams, in addition to the first team—and he had never encountered that name before. So who was this player?

He looked across at the Rangers bench and spotted the unfamiliar face. The lad looked like he was fresh out of school. Fancy Ian Fox taking a gamble on a sixteen-year-old in one of the most crucial games of his career!

Swinton knew about Robbie Clarke's arm break, but surely there were other squad players who could deputize for Dennis Jensen on the subs bench, without resorting to someone who was entirely untested at this level?

Down on the bench, Nat watched as the Wildman called the team together for a huddle and a last pep talk before kick-off. He could hear the Wildman's growl but not his actual words. The circle then broke up, with the Wildman shaking his fist at everyone to fire them up even further. Rangers won the toss and the Wildman opted to play from the Shipper End for the first half.

The ref checked with his two assistants, who both waved their flags in return. Nat said a silent prayer, one that this time was as much about himself as it was about the team. If anyone had told him a few weeks ago that he'd be on the subs bench for the Rangers vs. Tottenham game, he'd have laughed like a deranged hyena.

The first twenty minutes were a tense affair with few

chances. Tottenham were twelfth in the Premier League, so they didn't have an acute sense of having to play for something, but their manager, Graham Stokes, was an old-school tough guy and never accepted anything less than total commitment from his players.

In the twenty-third minute, a great raking pass from Corragio found Adilson on the edge of the penalty area. He trapped the ball with his left instep and hit it with his right foot. It was an excellent strike and flew straight past Brad Short into the Tottenham goal. Nat was immediately on his feet with the rest of the stadium.

"A goal for Rangers!" boomed the announcer's voice. "Scored by number seven—ADILSON!"

The cheers shook the stands, so great was the joy, not to mention relief, of the home crowd. After being mobbed by the team, Adilson ran over to the bench and bowed to Fox.

"Excellent work, son!" shouted Fox, thumping the air with delight.

"Get a move on!" shouted the referee, prompting Adilson to run off for the restart.

Tottenham dominated the next period, but their direct shooting chances were limited by the brilliant positional play of the back four and Sacrois, who made two superb sliding tackles. Lee Carshalton had a blistering free kick saved by a fully stretched Chris Webb, but a minute later the ref blew for half-time.

Fox was the first into the tunnel, with Evans hurrying behind him.

Nat piled into the locker room with the other players. The mood was almost upbeat, but people knew to their cost the folly of early celebrations.

"I'm not going to change anything," Fox told the players. "You've been brilliant—you've done exactly what I've asked of you. You've pretty much kept Carshalton out of the game. He looks down. Keep on him and his head will drop completely. I want you all to go out there and do more of the same. Keep the passes clean and simple.

"Adilson, you took that goal brilliantly. Keep on testing Short whenever you get a shooting opportunity. If we get a second goal, we'll batten down the hatches and play for the win. Everyone OK?"

"Yes, boss!" chorused the players.

Tottenham came out with renewed vigor for the second half, and five minutes in, Chris Webb had to make an acrobatic save to deny a Keith Devonshire belter. Emi then went close from a corner and Paolo Corragio had an effort hacked off the Tottenham goal line.

Then in the seventy-first minute, Tottenham struck. Kelvin was wrong-footed by Carshalton, who advanced into the penalty area and curled a shot around the outstretched Webb. The Tottenham fans went berserk. The Rangers fans were silenced with an agonizing sense of déjà vu.

Fox was immediately on his feet, pacing up and down the technical area with an agitated expression on his face. The Rangers players desperately tried to raise their game, but the Tottenham goal had crushed their spirits. Once again, they'd given away a lead. As the player who'd let Carshalton in, Kelvin was mortified. The Wildman kept on shouting positive stuff at him, but Kelvin's concentration had been badly affected. Fox quickly pulled Kelvin off and sent on Dave Swan in his place. Kelvin disappeared down the tunnel by himself.

The next twelve minutes were agony to watch. Tottenham, sensing the deflation of the Rangers players, came at them like vultures, firing shots in from everywhere. Webb was incredibly busy, both saving these attempts and screaming at his defense to do their job properly.

As the clock turned onto the eighty-sixth minute, Fox looked at Nat.

"Get your kit on," said the manager. "I'm taking Jensen off."

For a second, Nat couldn't comprehend what Fox had told him—it was like he was speaking a different language. But instinctively he did what he was told. Off came the tracksuit. He left his seat and hurried down to the sidelines with Fox beside him. Fox grabbed the assistant referee's attention and told him about the switch.

With adrenaline crashing through his veins, Nat did some quick stretches and jumps.

This cannot be happening!

The assistant got the attention of the ref and held up his electronic board. As a Tottenham player kicked the ball out of play, the ref nodded for the substitution to take place.

"Substitution for Rangers!" came the announcement. "Coming off—number fourteen, Dennis Jensen. Dennis will be replaced by number thirty-three, Nat Dixon!"

47

You're On

"I want you to just go for it," said Fox into Nat's ear. "Get out there and play your normal game."

Jensen ran off and slapped both of Nat's palms. "Good luck," he mouthed.

The assistant referee gave Nat a nod. And Nat ran on.

The crowd responded with cheers and murmurs. No one was expecting an unknown to grace the stadium, especially this late in the season.

For his first couple of minutes, Nat just ran. He ran into the Tottenham half when Corragio hoofed the ball up there. He ran to the right wing when Adilson was there calling for support. He ran back into the Rangers half when Tottenham set out on another attack. And then, before he knew it, the ball was at his feet. It was as if his whole life had been geared toward this one second. He controlled it with the bottom of his left boot and passed it cleanly to Emi.

I've done it. My first ever pass in the Premier League.

And I didn't give it away.

For the next two minutes, the play was all out on the left and then, after some serious time-wasting by the Tottenham defense, Adilson managed to pry the ball away. He evaded a couple of tackles and then hit a long pass to Nat, who was on the right, about twenty yards outside the penalty area. Nat knew instantly what he was going to do. Steve Townsend was parallel with the last Tottenham defender. Nat's pass was deadly accurate. Townsend collected it and sprinted into the penalty area. It was Townsend versus the keeper. Every supporter rose to their feet, willing Townsend to score. He pulled his leg back and ... booted it over. There were agonized cries of disappointment as a ballboy threw a new ball onto the field. Nat stared at Townsend.

That was a sitter. How could he have missed it?

A minute later, Short whacked a goal kick well into Rangers' penalty area. It was a nothing ball. But Dean Jobson panicked and sliced the ball. It went to Corragio, who failed to control it, and then, seemingly out of nowhere, Lee Carshalton was onto it. He bore down on Chris Webb and smacked the ball under the keeper's body.

"NOOOO!" screamed thirty thousand Rangers fans. A moment later, the final whistle went—Rangers 1, Tottenham 2. Luckily, Wigan and Bolton had both lost, but Sunderland had gotten a point at Fulham, so they were now level with Rangers, and were only at the bottom of the table because Rangers' goal difference was a fraction better than theirs.

Wigan	30 points
Bolton	30 points
Hatton Rangers	27 points
Sunderland	27 points

The locker room was like a morgue. It was cold and silent and miserable. The players sat on the benches, their faces betraying the agony of the afternoon. Relegation suddenly felt like a bulky and uncomfortable item of clothing the team would be forced to wear.

The silence was broken by Paolo Corragio. He shot a filthy glare at Dean Jobson. "If you hadn't screwed up that goal kick, we'd have gotten a point," he seethed.

Jobson stared back at him, as did all the other players.

"What did you say?" demanded Jobson, his face taut with anger.

"You kicked at it like we were in immediate danger."

"Well, you totally failed to control it!" snapped Jobson.

"Leave it!" ordered the Wildman.

"Your lousy control could send us down!" shouted Jobson.

Corragio was on his feet in an instant. His face was purple with rage. The veins on his neck stood out like tiny frozen worms. He charged at Jobson, who was also now on his feet. Jobson's face was red too, his breathing fast and furious. But Corragio was quicker. He pushed into Jobson, making him stagger backward, but as he did so, he lashed out with his foot and caught Corragio in the stomach. Corragio bent double in pain.

Nat stared at the unfolding scene in absolute horror. The next moment, everything went completely crazy. The Wildman sprang up and grabbed Jobson, who was getting ready for another attack. Chris Webb leaped onto Corragio and pulled him away.

"GET OFF ME!" shrieked Jobson, his fists flailing, his voice hoarse and incensed.

"Want another try, loser?" yelled Corragio, who was now struggling with Webb.

Jobson flung the Wildman off and dived back toward Corragio. But Adilson and Emi jumped in his way.

"It was your fault!" shrieked Corragio.

Jobson was now trying to get past the Wildman, Robbie Clarke and Pierre Sacrois. He was fighting like crazy, using fists, shoulders, elbows, and legs. Andy Young had joined Webb in holding Corragio back.

"WHAT ON EARTH IS GOING ON?" a voice suddenly bellowed, rising above the entire changing-room din.

It was Ian Fox. He had just walked into the room and he stood there, frozen with shock, fists clenched tightly. Instantly, the shouting and fighting stopped.

The other players let go of Jobson and Corragio.

"I'm appalled!" shouted Fox. "Two players from my club fighting each other! It's a complete disgrace. Sit down, all of you! NOW!"

The players shuffled back onto the benches. Jobson held a hand up to his face in an attempt to staunch the bleeding.

Fox walked over and stood in front of the team, his body shaking with anger. "Never have I seen anything like this!" he seethed, his voice a low guttural growl. "No one, repeat NO ONE, fights on my watch. I know you're desperately upset about the result, but that's what it is, one result. As you're all aware, I NEVER give up until the final whistle of the final game. We've got two more matches and if we get enough points we can stay up. And it's not just down to us—everyone else's results count. The relegation zone is packed. It's not over."

Jobson and Corragio were looking down at the ground.

"I want you all changed and out of here. Go home. See your wives and girlfriends and families. Watch TV, read the paper, play with your kids. Tomorrow is a new day and we start with a clean slate. Does every single person in the room get what I'm saying?"

"Yes, boss," everyone muttered.

"Good." Fox nodded. "Dean and Paolo, you two stay behind. We're sorting this thing out between you, here and now. I will not let anything like this happen, ever again!"

Nat stared at the two combatants.

Can Fox really fix their hatred? If other players hadn't stepped in, they'd have ripped large pieces out of each other.

Everyone changed quickly. No one showered—they didn't want to linger. They could see how vital it was for Fox to be barricaded in the locker room with Jobson and Corragio. Emi invited Nat back to his place; Nat thanked him but said no. He just wanted some head space. His dad was waiting for him at the front of the stadium. As they walked back to the car, Nat's mind rang with one thought.

We don't need bankruptcy to smash Hatton Rangers apart. We're doing it to ourselves.

48

The Press Pack

There were several raised eyebrows in Rangers' media suite when Ian Fox walked in for the post-match press conference. For the last four games he'd sent Stan Evans to deputize for him. Various experienced journalists believed he'd been doing this because he'd lost his nerve or was just resigned to relegation.

"Good to see you again, Ian!" someone called out.

"I wish I could say the same about you all!" quipped Fox.

There was general laughter in the room as Fox took his place behind the table and the reporters made sure they had their pens, microphones, and TV cameras at the ready.

"Gentlemen," began Fox, scanning the room, "and ladies," he added, spying two female reporters—one a print journalist, the other from BBC Radio. "I've got fifteen minutes with you, because if I'm not home on time tonight, my wife's going to kill me! So we might as well get started."

Everyone laughed loudly.

"Go on, Danny, you go first," declared Fox at the raised hands of the media folk.

"Danny Short, *Sunday Mirror*," said the reporter by way of introduction to the room. "How disappointed are you with today's result?"

"I'm beyond disappointment," replied Fox. "It was agony out there."

"Harry Dodds, *Mail on Sunday*. What action are you going to take against Jobson and Corragio? We've heard they were fighting in the locker room after the game."

"I'm not going to comment on that, Harry. All I will say is: there is a minimum standard of behavior I expect from anyone who represents this club, and that standard was not met this afternoon."

"Ray Swinton, *Sunday Crest*. Who on earth is Nat Dixon, Mr. Fox? He's got a squad number, you used him as a sub, but I, for one, have never heard of him."

There were nods of assent around the room.

"I'm glad you asked that," answered Fox, "and I'm happy to explain Nat's situation to you. The lad was spotted at the end of last year, playing street soccer in the States. Stan Evans was on a scouting mission and chanced upon him. He thought the Dixon boy was too good to let go, so when we heard his family was moving back to the UK we signed him in the January transfer window."

"Where has he been since then?" demanded Swinton. "It's May. I certainly haven't seen him at any training sessions, or anywhere else for that matter."

"You know how it is, Ray." Fox smiled. "We signed him within the deadline, but his paperwork has taken ages to be fully processed. We only completed the last formalities a couple of weeks ago and that's the reason for his seemingly sudden appearance. He's totally legitimate—you can check his registration papers. We just had to do things by the book; we had to be patient."

"Kelly Drayton, BBC Radio. How do you feel about the three other teams in the bottom four losing today?"

As Fox responded to this question, Ray Swinton was thinking about Fox's reply to his. It sounded plausible, and everyone else in the room seemed to accept it. But something about it didn't quite ring true. He doodled a couple of goal nets on his notepad. But then again, maybe he was reading too much into it. Maybe it was exactly as Fox said. He looked up and made himself focus on the next question and Fox's answer.

49

Newsprint Heaven

Dave walked out onto the back porch, carrying the most enormous pile of newsprint Nat had ever seen.

"I've got all the Sunday papers." Dave grinned. "And the *Jewish News*, just in case. Spent an absolute fortune, but it was well worth it. It's not every day your son gets his first mention in the national press."

"Do they mention me?" asked Nat, leaping up and grabbing the *Sunday Times* from the top of the pile. This paper named him as one of the subs but no more, as did the *Mail on Sunday*, the *Observer* and the *Sunday Telegraph*. There was nothing in the *Jewish News*, but then as he'd changed his name from Levy to Dixon, he probably wasn't on their radar just yet. But Ray Swinton's match report in the *Sunday Crest* was different. Nat scanned forward to the relevant paragraph:

> ... Coming on in the eighty-sixth minute was sixteen-year-old Nat Dixon, a new face at the club, discovered in the US by Rangers' assistant manager, Stan Evans. Dixon had few touches, but he didn't seem overawed by the occasion and I think we might be seeing more of him at some stage in the future ...

One paragraph—that was all, but Nat and Dave read it and reread it over and over again.

"There you go!" said his dad, giving Nat a tight hug. "No questions about your age! You're in there!"

Nat had to admit that it did feel good to see his United States cover story in black and white. Swinton also had the whole of the facing page with a big interview with Chris Webb. It began thus:

Relegation, failure, disaster. These aren't words that enter Hatton Rangers keeper Chris Webb's lexicon. Webb, a stalwart in the Rangers goal for the last ten years, is not interested in the possibility of his side's demotion to the second tier.

"I ignore all of the R-word talk," he told the *Sunday Crest*. "I've always been a one-match-at-a-time player, and I judge the team by how well they performed in the last game."

But pressed on what he'd do if Rangers were relegated, Webb was very clear in his answer.

"I'm a Rangers player; I'm on a three-year contract. I love the club. I love the fans. Why should I move on? Because someone dangles some more money in my face or says their club is more glamorous? The obscene riches on offer in the game don't interest me. I play because I love the game; the money is just a bonus to me. If we do go down, we fight as hard as we can next season and we come straight back up."

"I've always thought highly of Chris Webb," said Dave, reading over Nat's shoulder. "A real mensch. If more players were like him, the game would be in far better shape."

Nat and his dad stretched out on the porch and started to make their way through the rest of the papers. They devoured the sports sections and then Dave checked out the news and Nat went for the arts sections. After that Nat read a long magazine article about the world's most elusive diamond thief and then closed his eyes and had a snooze.

The rest of the day was spent in much the same way. They read the papers, ate, listened to the radio, ate again. When Dad brought out his harmonica, Nat retreated inside.

50

A Violent Clash

"I don't need to tell you how important Wednesday's game at Liverpool is. We've got them at Anfield and then Man United at home on Sunday for the season's last game. You could say these will be the most important days in the club's history."

It was Monday morning at Shelton Park. Ian Fox was standing on one of the training ground's fields addressing his players, who were taking a breather, sipping from bottles of water and looking up at him.

"They'll come at us like attack dogs," continued Fox. "They play with bravado and panache at Anfield—most of you have played up there before and you know what it's like."

I know and I've only seen them on TV.

"And in Phil Sutton and Dino Simic, they have two of the best attacking players in the world right now. These guys are lethal, particularly from set plays. Wildman and Emi, you'll have your hands full. Andy and Kelvin, you'll need to double up, and I want two people on the goal line to support Webby—that's Paolo and Dean."

Nat shot a sideways look at Jobson and Corragio. They were standing right next to each other with no indication that they'd had a massive bust-up just the other day. Ian

Fox had obviously worked some of his diplomatic magic on them. Either that, or he'd threatened to fire them.

"Won't that leave players unmarked?" asked Andy Young.

"It's a risk we'll have to take," responded Fox. "I've seen how many headers they glance in against teams whose goalkeepers are left exposed. No, we'll pack the goal line and take our chances. Once they've had a couple of efforts blocked, they'll get frustrated. When they get frustrated they sometimes start to unravel. And Simic has a foul temper; he's easily agitated."

"You want us to hassle him?" asked Adilson.

"No," replied Fox, "just make him feel uncomfortable, don't give him any space and he'll get upset all by himself."

There were nods between various players. Simic had scored the only goal in Rangers' 1–0 home defeat to Liverpool earlier in the season. Wednesday night was payback time.

"So the plan is to defend, not too deeply—stop them getting too near for shooting—and then hit them on the break. Adilson is faster than all of their defenders so he's the one you should be aiming for. And Adilson"—the manager looked at his Brazilian star—"no need to be extra flashy. I know you love your step-overs and your balletics, but the main path in this game is Route One. Beat their full-backs and play it—on the ground—to Dennis and Steve. As we did for the Arsenal game in February, Dennis is going to play behind Steve. Steve, your job is to hold up that ball and play off Dennis and Adilson. When we're in promising positions I want Pierre and Paolo to push up too. Dean, you stay put and clear up if we lose the ball. I want you snapping at their heels, OK?"

Dean Jobson nodded.

"Why do I have to be up there alone?" demanded Steve Townsend. "Against Liverpool I'll be wasting my time. You know what happens: there's all of this talk about hitting them on the break, but when the ball actually does break, it'll just be me up there, surrounded by red shirts. We'll never score. I think we should play with a four-four-two formation. That will give the team more shape."

Fox exchanged a glance with Evans. "Thanks for that, Steve," said Fox, barely managing to contain his anger. "It's always good to hear your opinions on team structure and tactics, but unfortunately for you on this occasion, the decision has already been made by the powers that be, i.e. me."

"I know what I'm talking about," simmered Townsend. "You're making a big mistake."

Fox ignored him and continued. "For the next hour I want to work on set pieces with the Wildman, Emi, Andy, Kelvin, and Webby. Paolo and Deano—you're on the line, as I mentioned. Steve and Dennis, I want you to be Sutton and Simic. Adilson and Nat are going to be Liverpool's wide men—Jones and Rutherford—the guys who support Simic and Sutton. They're technically wingers, but sometimes they play like two extra center-forwards. And they're quick."

Townsend muttered something under his breath.

"What was that?" demanded Fox irritably.

"Nothing." Townsend scowled.

"Good." Fox nodded. "The rest of you are working with Stan. Let's go!"

He clapped his hands and all of the players rose to their feet. Steve Townsend looked particularly sulky, even by his miserable standards.

Chris Webb took up his place in goal, with Jobson and Corragio on either side of him on the line. Fox began floating corners into the box. Townsend and Jensen went for every ball, with Andy and Emi on Townsend and the Wildman and Kelvin on Jensen. Nat and Adilson hung back a little to pick up any scraps that were fed to them. Despite Townsend and Jensen's best efforts, the defensive unit acted brilliantly, thwarting every effort. Dean Jobson and Corragio headed, chested and kicked away several goal-bound efforts.

"Looks like the boss has gotten some of the tactics right, doesn't it, Steve?" said the Wildman to Townsend. Townsend spat on the ground and turned away.

Then Nat and Adilson were given the task of running at the pretend Liverpool defense. Nat made a couple of twisting runs and played some decent balls to the strikers.

"Good work, Nat!" Fox shouted after one spinning pass that reached Jensen's head.

When Fox was satisfied with his defensive unit, he brought everyone back together again and organized some one-touch four vs. four games. In the first of these, Nat was playing in the same team as Townsend, who shut him out—never passing to him. But in the second, he came into his own. He exchanged some crisp passes with Jensen and netted a couple of close-range goals. Evans gave him a thumbs-up.

Toward the end of the third game he was involved in, with Townsend on the opposing side this time, Nat rifled a pass through to Dean Jobson and was running to get the return, when he felt a searing pain in his left ankle. He winced and crashed onto the turf.

"What the heck was that?" yelled the Wildman, running over to the deliverer of this vicious tackle—Steve Townsend.

Townsend held his hands in the air. "I played the ball," he said without a trace of guilt. "Too bad he couldn't take the challenge."

Nat held his ankle and ground his teeth. It hurt badly, but nothing was broken. He hobbled to his feet. The Wildman and Emi were standing next to Townsend, looking furious.

"You're totally out of line!" shouted Emi. "You could have snapped his ankle in two!"

"Well I didn't, did I?" Townsend sneered. "Now can we get on with the game?"

The Wildman jabbed a finger at Townsend. "I'm warning you, Steve," he seethed. "Play another stunt like that and you won't know what's hit you!"

"Ooh!" exclaimed Townsend with an exaggerated high-pitched squeal. "I'm so scared!"

"Are you OK?" Kelvin asked Nat, as Townsend sauntered off, looking a picture of innocence.

"I'm fine," replied Nat, "it looked worse than it was."

"It looked like exactly what it was," fumed the Wildman. "I've got a good mind to punch that guy's lights out."

"Not a great idea," said Fox, coming over and standing among his players. "I've had enough fighting for two lifetimes. We need everyone fit for Wednesday night, even those with anger-management issues."

This alleviated the tension somewhat. Several people looked at Steve Townsend's retreating back and laughed.

"Right," said Fox, "we'll finish now for the morning. We'll take an hour for lunch and then I want everyone in the gym, following the programs Stan has devised for you. We'll then have another short session out here and call it a day."

As Nat limped across the field with Emi, he couldn't help noticing the unmistakable smirk on Steve Townsend's face.

Nat sat down on a chair in the main treatment room. Colin Dempsey, the club physiotherapist, knelt down and took a good look at his ankle.

"It's just bruised," he assured Nat, "but I'm going to put an ice pack on it to reduce any swelling. How did it happen?"

"Stiff challenge from Steve Townsend," replied Nat.

Dempsey stood up and made a face. "Why doesn't that surprise me?" he huffed, walking over to the freezer and pulling out a curved pack of blue ice. He came back and applied it to Nat's ankle.

"It's not the first time he's gone in hard in training," said Dempsey, "and the funny thing is, he always goes for the other strikers, never a defender or a midfielder. Bit of a coincidence?"

Nat shrugged his shoulders. However much he hated Steve Townsend, he didn't want to go bad-mouthing him to the club staff, at least not yet.

"Right," announced Dempsey. "Keep that applied to your ankle for the next half-hour. I'll come back then to have another quick look. There are some magazines on the table."

He pulled a small table toward Nat. It was laden with style magazines. Nat picked one up—*Subterfuge*. Dempsey left the room and Nat flicked through its pages. If you wanted to buy a yacht or sky-dive in the Caribbean, then *Subterfuge* was clearly the magazine for you. And then Nat had a thought.

Maybe if I make it here, really make it, I'll be able to buy my own yacht! Or go skydiving in the Caribbean. But then again, maybe not.

He closed his eyes and had a vision of Copa Cabana beach. A little bit of soccer on the sand would do. He'd make his way back to Rio in the not-too-distant future, he was determined.

The Challenge

"You've got to be joking!"

Steve Townsend barged straight into Ian Fox's office, the squad sheet grasped in his hand—the same squad sheet he'd ripped off the changing-room wall when he'd read it two minutes ago.

"Thanks for knocking, Steve," snapped Fox furiously. "What is it?"

"This!" exclaimed Townsend, slamming the sheet down on Fox's desk.

Fox looked at it. "The squad sheet for tomorrow's game?"

"Yeah," shouted Townsend. "What on earth is that Dixon kid doing on there? You can't be serious about sticking him in for the Liverpool game. It's too big a game. We need experience out there, not some nervy little kid."

"Sorry, Steve," said Fox, eyeing his striker with distaste, "but since when is it your responsibility to pick the squad? I don't see your name on the manager's door!"

"Come on, boss. We can't afford to carry inexperience for this match. It's crazy!"

Fox stood up, walked to the door and stood beside it. "This is my office door," he said. "I want you to walk through it and get out of my sight in the next ten seconds or it will be YOU who doesn't travel with us to Liverpool. One, two, three…"

Townsend shook his head furiously, muttered under his breath and stormed out.

"Lovely to see you too, Steve," said Fox to the empty room, before shutting the door again.

52

Traveling in Style

Nat walked up the steps of the club bus, nodded hello to the driver, and stared open-mouthed at the vehicle's interior. He'd been on hundreds of coaches before, but this one was in a different league.

For a start, instead of just having forward-facing seats, the seats on here were grouped in fours, with two front-facing and two backward-facing, opposite each other. Sleek table lamps gave the cabin a mellow, relaxed feel. At the back was a kitchen area where staff were preparing trays laden with soft drinks and snacks. Individual entertainment units were set in the wall by every seat, boasting a host of computer games plus a range of films and TV shows.

This is unreal!

Dave had fretted a bit about the trip to Liverpool and had suggested that he drive up in the Mondeo and stay near the team in case Nat needed him. Nat had managed to dissuade him.

"Don't you think it would look slightly strange if one of Rangers' squad members nipped away from the team hotel to see his father?"

"Maybe," replied his dad. "So I'll just go to the match."

"It's OK, Dad, you don't have to. I know how hard

you're trying to find work, and taking a couple of days off is crazy. I'll be fine—I promise!"

"Over here!" called Kelvin, who'd nabbed a table for himself, Emi, and Adilson.

Nat walked up the aisle and stuffed his shoulder bag up on the luggage carrier. He slid down into his place and leaned back against the luxurious armchair-like seat.

On seeing Nat's awestruck expression, Emi laughed. "This is nothing!" He grinned. "Wait until you see the hotel. We stayed there last year—it's amazing!"

"Welcome to the kids' zone!" said Kelvin, smiling. "The boss, Evans, and the older guys all sit at the front and talk about their houses and their kids and their shares and other boring stuff like that!"

A steward wearing a name badge saying Anastasia stepped over to their table. "Afternoon, gentlemen, what can I get you?"

Being served drinks on a coach? I could get used to this!

"Can I have a Coke, please?" asked Emi. "Me, too," said Kelvin.

"And me, please," added Nat.

"A double whiskey for me," said Adilson, with a totally straight face.

Anastasia looked confused for a minute, but Kelvin and Emi burst out laughing. "He's only joking," said Kelvin. "He's strictly an apple-juice drinker."

Anastasia looked relieved and went to get the drinks. When she had handed them out she moved on to the next table.

"My dad played semi-pro," said Kelvin to the others. "And in those days they drank a lot, and I don't mean soft drinks. He wasn't that into alcohol, but some of his teammates drank like fish. Sometimes they'd drink at lunchtime on a match day. No wonder they could hardly kick the ball."

"I'm not anti-booze," mused Emi, "and on a night out I might have a couple of beers, but that's all. I can't see the point of getting drunk. It eventually takes its toll on your body."

"Right," announced Adilson, pulling out a pack of cards. "Shall we play poker first?"

"Definitely," agreed Emi and Adilson.

They all looked at Nat, who was very familiar with the game.

"We play for massive stakes," said Adilson. Nat was shocked.

"Only joking!" said Adilson thumping his arm. "Stakes are a pound so nobody loses much, especially not me. I'm the poker king!"

"In your dreams!" protested Kelvin.

They played for a long time and Nat got totally caught up in the game. He won some, he lost some, and when they decided to quit he was only down three pounds. After that, Adilson pulled out Nelson Mandela's *The Long Walk to Freedom* and told the others why it was one of the greatest books ever, while Nat, Emi, and Kelvin turned to their entertainment units.

Nat put on the headphones and flicked through some tunes on a Spotify playlist. There were lots he liked so he spent over an hour checking out various tracks. Then he played computer games and saw an old episode of *Fawlty Towers*, the classic 1970s British sitcom that his dad was always talking about. The episode was the one in which a rat was found in the hotel. Nat had seen the episode about a million times on cable in various locations around the globe, but he had to admit, it was still incredibly funny.

By 6 p.m. the coach was in Liverpool, and soon it pulled up in front of the hotel.

"Hang on a second," said Kelvin, looking out of the window, "this isn't where we stayed last year—that was Sovereign House. This is called the Lantern."

"Can I have your attention, please!" boomed out Ian Fox's voice. He was standing at the front of the coach.

"You may have noticed we're not going to Sovereign House this year," he explained, "and the reason is simple—cash. We're trying to trim the budget as much as possible so we're staying here at the Lantern. It's perfectly adequate for our needs."

"It looks like a dive," muttered Steve Townsend sourly.

"Stop whining, Townsend," snapped the Wildman sharply.

Townsend scowled at the captain.

The players piled off the coach and into the small lobby of the Lantern. It smelled of disinfectant and had fading light-blue paint and an old-fashioned rotating wooden fan on the ceiling.

Stan Evans spoke to the woman at the front desk and started handing out keys. Everyone had to share. Emi and Kelvin were rooming together, so Nat was given Adilson as a roommate, a situation that pleased him.

"Come on, man!" said Adilson, grabbing his suitcase and running toward the lift. "Let's go check it out."

At times Adilson was like a big kid. That was part of why Nat liked him; he was fun. Their room was on the second floor. It had two single beds and a bathroom and was covered in pale-yellow wallpaper. A small, old-fashioned TV sat on a table. Adilson flopped down on the bed nearest the door.

"Nowhere near as cool as Sovereign House," he said, "but a bed is a bed."

At 7:30 they ate supper with the rest of the squad in the hotel's small restaurant. They were the only guests staying at the hotel, so they had the place to themselves. Nat sat with Emi, Kelvin, Adilson, and Andy Young. The plates weren't spotlessly clean and the fish could have been presented in a more appealing fashion, but no one complained—they didn't want a run-in with Ian Fox just before such a massive game. Dessert was lots of different kinds of fruit, sliced up and served on large platters.

As the meal was winding down, Ian Fox stood up and everyone else fell silent.

"We're not going to have any big team talk tonight.

We've discussed this game enough at the training ground," he began. "I will be reminding some of you individually tomorrow about your specific roles. I just want to reinforce the fact that Liverpool are beatable. That's not some mad theory, it's a fact. Blackburn came here in November and beat them 2–1. Arsenal visited in February and clocked up a 2–0 victory. Keep those games in your mind before we run out there tomorrow. On our day, we're as good as any other team in the Premier League. We just need to give it a hundred percent commitment. Do you get me?"

"Yes, boss," replied the players in unison.

After supper, the players split into groups. Some went to the lounge to watch TV, a couple read books. Steve Townsend slipped out of the hotel and didn't come back until much later. Nat, Emi, Kelvin, and Adilson went to the games room and played pool. The pool table's green baize had a couple of rips in its surface but it was easily playable. Pool was a game Nat loved. Dad was a decent player and had taught him well. He saw instantly that Emi and Adilson were pretty good and that Kelvin was excellent. They played for ages, sipping from bottles of mineral water, chatting and joking.

At 10 p.m. Ian Fox did his rounds.

"Nighty night!" he said to the pool boys, "and no midnight feasts, you guys! I need you all fresh for tomorrow. So off you go!"

Nat said goodnight to Emi and Kelvin, and then he and Adilson went back to their room.

They lay on their respective beds and Adilson flicked through the TV channels.

"This is rubbish!" He laughed. "They don't even have cable."

Nat wasn't bothered. His mind was filled with one thing: tomorrow night's game at Anfield.

Anfield

The following morning after breakfast, the coach picked up the Hatton Rangers party and drove them to Sires Park—a private training ground used by several local teams—which they had booked for the day. It had one full-sized grass field. After some stretches, jogging, and sprinting, they split into positional groups. Stan Evans took the strikers.

He threw ball after ball at them, telling them first to catch them on the volley, then on the half volley, then with one touch followed by a volley. They did this in front of an empty net. Nat did well in these tasks, consistently striking the ball cleanly and hard, and finding the net.

They moved on to headers: headers from free kicks, headers from corners, long-range headers, short-range headers. Next, everyone met up again and they played a series of ten-minute five-a-side games. Nat made a couple of goals and scored with a cracking volley.

They ate a light lunch at the training ground's café and, when they'd digested their meal, did some more running and passing exercises. The coach then took them back to the hotel. Several players, including Adilson, took a nap. Nat watched an old black-and-white heist movie on TV and finished reading his Ed McBain thriller.

At 4:15 p.m. the coach arrived again, and this time it

drove through the streets of Liverpool and transported them to Anfield. As they approached the famous ground, Nat gazed out the window at the stadium. Compared to the Ivy, it was vast. It towered over you like an intimidating bully. Nat felt a nervous thrill. This whole enterprise was getting more serious by the minute. This was Anfield, for God's sake.

The bus drove through the Liverpool players' parking lot and under a steel shutter that led into a huge parking area below the stadium. Everyone piled off and headed for the away-team locker room.

Wherever you looked as you walked down the corridors, you saw Liverpool history: a history of winning trophies— the old First Division, the FA Cup, those famous European Cups. Giant photos of Liverpool legends stared down at you: Tommy Smith, Emlyn Hughes, Ian St. John, John Barnes, Ian Rush, Kevin Keegan, Kenny Dalglish, Fernando Torres. This incredible past made Rangers seem like a youth league team in comparison.

They filed into the locker room and took their time getting changed. Ian Fox and Stan Evans made their way among everyone, an encouraging word here, a tactical reminder there. Nat looked up when Fox tapped him on the shoulder and sat down beside him.

"I'm not sure if you'll get any action today," began Fox. "It's a massive game and I don't want to take any chances."

Nat nodded. This was exactly what he'd been expecting to hear.

"However," Fox went on, "if you do get a chance, I want you to remember a couple of things. Their goalie, Joe Hodgson, sometimes strays off his line. I've seen him do it several times. It's as if he can't bear being away from the action and is drawn a few yards out of his safety zone. It's a weakness, Nat, and one that's worth thinking about. The other thing is that their defenders aren't the fastest in the league. These guys can be sold dummies and can be left floundering if you turn suddenly or keep the ball down and play an unexpected ball into the area. All right?"

"Yes, boss." Nat nodded. He had listened to Fox's every word as if he were a learned rabbi passing on pearls of great wisdom.

"Good." Fox smiled. "Just keep them in your mind."

At 7:15 the Rangers players walked out to the mostly empty stadium and did some stretches, some running routines and got the feel of the field. The grass had just been cut and, considering how far into the season they were, it was in incredible condition. Nat tried not to look up at the vast stands of the famous Kop end, or the thousands of fans who were streaming in. He had to focus on the ball—nothing else mattered.

They then returned to the locker room and got into their jerseys.

As the kick-off neared, Fox gave them a last-minute pep talk.

"Don't forget what's at stake," he said quietly. "You, me, all of our jobs could be on the line here. So this isn't an ordinary football match. It's a battle for survival. Go out there, acknowledge our traveling supporters, and for them, and for every single person who's paid to see us this season, get the job done."

"YES!" shouted the players, fired up by Fox's words and ready for the start.

Both sets of players were called out of their locker rooms. They lined up next to each other. The Wildman hugged the Liverpool captain Archie MacBride; they'd played together in their early days at Scunthorpe. Nat gazed at the Liverpool players in awe. There was Sutton, there was Simic—two of the best strikers in the game. They were giants and Nat's spirits sank as he considered the reality of Rangers trying to contain these guys.

How can we compete with them on an equal footing?

Then it was time to move.

54

Kicking Off

Both lines proceeded down the tunnel, studs clanking on the concrete floor. Nat saw the world-famous sign: "This is Anfield."

In a time-honored tradition, all of the Liverpool players touched the sign for good luck. The Rangers players pretended not to notice, but Nat could see that even the sign intimidated everyone, with the possible exception of the Wildman and Chris Webb.

Running out onto the field, the players were greeted by a vast crescendo of noise, the Liverpool fans in fine singing voice, their songs and chants echoing around the entire stadium. The Hatton Rangers traveling fans tried to make themselves heard, but they had no chance.

Nat took his place on the bench and went through his ritual of saying a prayer to himself. He really hoped it would work this time, but, as he looked again at the two Liverpool forwards, he shuddered. Phil Sutton was the most in-form striker in the Premier League, with twenty-six goals to his name this season and three call-ups to the England squad. The Croatian Dino Simic was also in blistering form, with five goals in the last two games. And the rest of the side wasn't too bad either.

Sutton and Simic didn't take long to make an impact.

From the first Liverpool corner in the seventh minute, Simic rose above everyone to smash a powerful header against the post. The ball shot straight at Sutton, whose powerful volley skimmed the crossbar. The Rangers players breathed deep sighs of relief and regrouped—the Wildman yelling them on and demanding that they focus. At twenty-six minutes, Dennis Jensen evaded the Liverpool offside trap, but scuffed his shot.

And then, just before half-time, Liverpool scored. Their Scottish central-midfielder and captain, Archie MacBride, picked out Sutton with a long, raking pass. He dummied a shot and squared to an unmarked Simic, who slotted it home.

Ian Fox went completely crazy. "NO ONE PICKED HIM UP!" he screamed, running to the edge of the technical area and shaking his fists at his forlorn defenders. Two minutes later the whistle went for half-time. Fox ushered his players off the field urgently, running beside them to the away locker room. He needed to get at them— needed to shore up the leaky defense and convince his team they could still get something out of the match.

"YOU'RE BETTER THAN THIS!" he yelled at a silent locker room. "Every one of you is a strong player. Every one of you has something special. Forget about our league position. Forget where we are. Concentrate on your own game and we'll get back into this!"

Once again, another Fox rant inspired his players and they went out for the second half, determined to make amends for the first-half slippage. Adilson in particular was outstanding. He took Liverpool players on and beat them with his skill and speed. His passes were outrageously ambitious, but ninety percent of them came off. He shouted for a penalty in the sixty-sixth minute, when it looked like he'd been felled by Liverpool's left-back, Kurt Schuster, but the ref waved play on. Fox and Evans were on their feet, waving their arms and screaming, but when did that kind of protest ever change a ref's mind?

Fox was chewing his gum so hard, Nat wouldn't have been surprised if his mouth developed its own motor and sped off somewhere. On seventy-five minutes, Fox grabbed Nat's shoulder.

"I'm taking Jensen off. Get changed!"

Nat's heart leaped wildly. He took his cue and thirty seconds later he was changed and jumping up and down on the sidelines.

The Kop immediately broke out into a song of "Who's the kid?"

"Block 'em out!" commanded Fox.

Nat tried, but it wasn't possible.

When the assistant referee held up his electronic board, the Rangers fans stood and clapped. Jensen ran off and slapped palms with Nat. And then Nat was on. He felt the hallowed turf of Anfield beneath his cleats.

For his first five minutes on the field, he did nothing but run into space and shout for the ball. But it never reached him. A couple of times it found Steve Townsend, who gave it away on one occasion and shot wildly on the other.

And then a flighted pass from Dean Jobson landed at Nat's feet. Simic ran in on him, but Nat shielded the ball, turned quickly and was off. He made a short pass to Corragio, who returned the ball. Nat sidestepped another Liverpool challenge and bore down on the penalty area. He looked up and saw Joe Hodgson standing a couple of yards off his line—just as Fox had told him! Nat immediately smacked the ball. It floated through the air and caught Hodgson by surprise. He stumbled backward and just managed to push it over the bar.

Suddenly the Rangers fans had something to cheer about. Adilson took the corner, a beautiful in-swinger. Hodgson jumped and attempted to punch it, but missed it completely. Steve Townsend leaped with a clear sight of goal, but headed it wide. The look of disgust on the Wildman's face needed no explanation.

Nat was then part of a quick passing move that involved six Rangers players, but it was stifled at the edge of the penalty area and trickled through to Hodgson. Nat took a quick look at the stadium clock.

Eighty-three minutes.

Rangers had just seven minutes to level things and grab a vital point.

Three minutes later, Adilson picked up the ball on the halfway line and passed it to Sacrois, who stroked it forward and then squared it to Jobson. Jobson ran a few yards and found Adilson, who was now running through the center channel. Adilson killed the ball with his left foot and passed it to Nat.

Nat began to run. Liverpool's tough guy, Ian Docherty, lunged at him, but he swerved around the vast aggressor and sprinted on. Seeing Adilson at the apex of the D, he found him with a perfect pass. Two Liverpool defenders scrambled toward Adilson, who passed straight back to Nat.

Knowing that the Liverpool defenders would run straight on to him, Nat turned his back to the goal and shielded the ball. As a defender slid in on either side of him, Nat sensed Adilson starting a run into the penalty area. In a split second, Nat back-heeled the ball in Adilson's direction.

It was a glorious pass, splitting the Liverpool defense and letting Adilson run on to goal, with only Hodgson to beat. Nat twisted around just in time to see Adilson go around the keeper and tuck the ball away.

Adilson pulled off his shirt and ran to the Rangers fans. The other Rangers players chased after him and leaped on him, screaming with delight. Nat jumped on top of the pile, shouting at the top of his voice. When the melee had subsided and the ref had cautioned Adilson for his shirt antics, the Brazilian ran over to Nat and gave him a huge hug.

"INCREDIBLE PASS!" yelled Adilson. "IT WAS BEAUTIFUL!"

"KEEP YOUR SHAPE!" shrieked a hoarse and very emotional Ian Fox.

There was only a minute left of normal time, plus there would be a few minutes of time added on. The Rangers obeyed Fox's command and kept things tight.

But in the third minute of time added on, Simic and Docherty combined brilliantly and sent Sutton rushing to the edge of the penalty area.

Nat was the nearest player. He acted instantly, lunging for the ball ... but completely missed it and brought Sutton down.

"PENALTY!" screamed every Liverpool fan. "SEND HIM OFF!" they yelled.

The foul was right on the edge of the area and Sutton had fallen inside the box.

Nat's heart thudded downward in his chest.

What have I done?

55

Seconds of Agony

What was the ref going to do? Was he going to give a penalty? Sutton NEVER missed from the spot. If it was a penalty, Rangers were sunk. Nat knew he was going to get a card, but would it be yellow or red? Sutton and Simic had been fairly level with each other, but would the ref rule that Sutton had been the last man?

The ref reached into his top pocket and to Nat's gut-crunching relief pulled out a yellow card. He brandished this at Nat and then quickly pointed to a spot a few inches outside the penalty area.

The Liverpool fans went mad with anger and dismay. What was the referee thinking of? It was a true cacophony of noise, like a crowd in a Roman amphitheater, and on this occasion, it was Nat who was the object of their hatred.

"You're lucky," mouthed Sutton with a sneer.

Chris Webb was already busy lining up his wall, holding up his fingers and screaming at his teammates.

"Ten yards!" declared the ref, spraying a line of foam to indicate exactly where he wanted the players to be. Nat stood on the goal line. He couldn't think what else to do. He would do anything to stop the ball crashing into the net and he reasoned that the goal line would give him the best opportunity of doing that. At that moment he felt that if it meant diving into the ball's path with his head and being hit so hard that he'd die—he'd do it!

Simic placed the ball down and took a few steps backward. His free kicks had vicious spin and lift and he'd scored some spectacular ones this season. Nat's body was so brittle with tension, he feared it might snap, but he bent his knees, ready to fling himself if necessary.

The ref blew his whistle and Simic ran to the ball, smacking it with the instep of his right boot. It soared above the wall and hurtled toward Webb's top right corner, but the Rangers keeper was already in mid-flight and with an athletic push, nudged the ball around the post and out for a corner.

Simic raced across the field to take the corner, but when he whacked it into the penalty area, Webb jumped above everyone else and caught the ball cleanly. He held it for a few seconds and then booted it skyward. Before it hit the turf, the ref blew the final whistle.

The Liverpool supporters rose and started leaving the ground muttering about Rangers' luck and a scoreline that in no way reflected the inequality of talent between their team and the west-of-London boys. The Rangers fans were dancing and chanting uproariously. A point at Anfield! How good was that?

And when the stadium announcer declared that Sunderland, Bolton, and Wigan had all lost, the Rangers fans went even crazier. Now Wigan and Bolton were only two points above Rangers.

Wigan	30 points
Bolton	30 points
Hatton Rangers	28 points
Sunderland	27 points

The Rangers players trotted over to their supporters and raised their arms aloft to applaud them. Nat saw the elation on the fans' faces and he clapped thunderously. Then the Rangers players waved their goodbyes and jogged off into the tunnel.

The joyful atmosphere back in the locker room was in stark contrast to the somber mood at half-time. Emi grabbed Nat and lifted him into the air.

"That back heel was outrageous!" He laughed. "Who do you think you are, Zinedine Zidane?"

Nat laughed back. "I just got lucky," he replied modestly.

"No way!" cried Emi. "It was inspirational!"

"He's right," said Kelvin coming over to give Nat a slap on the back. "It was absolutely brilliant—without it, Adilson would never have gone through!"

"Too right!" Dean Jobson called. "Good on you, kid!"

"Count me in on that!" shouted Andy Young.

Out of the corner of his eye, Nat spotted Steve Townsend scowling at him with contempt. Emi and Kelvin followed his gaze.

"Forget about him," said Emi. "The guy's well past it."

The Wildman then broke into song. "And it's Hatton

Rangers, Hatton Rangers FC. We're by far the greatest team the world has ever seen!"

Nat, along with everyone else, joined in enthusiastically. On and on the song went, rising in decibels each time they reached the beginning again. As the song finally wound down, Stan Evans popped his head around the door and beckoned to Nat. Nat's pants and socks and shoes were on already so he walked over, pulling on his T-shirt as he went.

"The gaffer wants to see you," said Evans.

Nat nodded. The praise from his teammates had been effusive. The boss would never go to their extremes, but even the most basic words of praise from the Rangers manager were worth a lot.

Evans led Nat down the hall toward a small room on the left-hand side. He ushered Nat in and then left. Fox was sitting behind a small desk and was on the phone. When he saw Nat enter, he wrapped up the call and stared at his youngest player for a few moments.

"What on earth were you playing at?" he hissed quietly.

Nat frowned. This was a strange opening for a speech of praise.

"I ... I don't ... I don't know what you mean," stammered Nat.

Fox stood up. "The foul on Sutton. It could have cost us the game!"

"But ... but it didn't," replied Nat with a crestfallen expression. "Chris Webb saved the free kick."

"That's not the point, Nat," fumed Fox, the anger fiery in his eyes. "You didn't have to bring him down."

"But he was through on goal!" protested Nat, the blood starting to pound between his ears. "He could have scored and we'd have lost the game."

"You weren't the last Rangers player!" snapped Fox. "The Wildman and Emi could have got to him. We were lucky they only got a free kick. A penalty would have killed us off."

"I thought I had to," insisted Nat. "I thought it was the only way to stop him!"

Fox put his fingers to the bridge of his nose and squeezed it. "Look, Nat," he said, trying to restore an element of calm to his voice. "I know you're only thirteen. I know it's me that put you in this situation. I know it's a baptism of fire for you. But when it comes to playing on the field, I have to treat you the way I treat all my other players. That's what we agreed. And if it was one of them who'd felled Sutton, I'd have them in here."

"But I made Adilson's goal and we got a point!" said Nat, his voice getting louder, tears stinging his eyes. "A point that could help save us!"

"I know," replied Fox, "but that doesn't take away from the recklessness of your challenge. If you're going to do that sort of thing every time I bring you on, our little project will end right now!"

Nat couldn't believe it. All of his good work in the game had been negated by that one foul. Talk about injustice!

"Go back to the team and think about what I've said," ordered Fox. "I've got enough on my plate without worrying about you conceding penalties in the dying seconds of every match."

"It was just a foul!" said Nat crossly.

"Go!" snapped Fox.

56

Spirits Down

Nat sat by himself on the coach journey back to London. Emi and Kelvin tried to get him involved in another game of cards, but he lied and said he was too tired to play. He didn't tell the others what had happened. He just sat there thinking about Fox's angry outburst. It was outrageous! What was wrong with the man? Rangers had been heading toward another defeat—another notch on the downward ladder to relegation and despair, but Nat had managed to help salvage something.

Instead of praising me for my back heel to Adilson, Fox goes and tells me off for giving away a foul that didn't even result in a goal!

Bitterness seeped through Nat's body.

Halfway through the journey he got a call from his dad.

"Am I speaking to the back-heel wonder boy?"

"Dad!" replied Nat, flushing with embarrassment.

"It was inspired! I'm still *kvelling*," gushed Dad. "And Adilson took it brilliantly!"

"Have you seen it?"

"No, it was on the radio. They played it about five times. You should hear the commentator. He went completely crazy!"

"I guess the pass came off," said Nat.

"Don't be so modest!" replied his dad. "You meant it, and it got through to him. We got a point. End of story."

"Anyway," said Nat, "how are you?"

"Fine, I'm actually at work. I got the Kellerton pharmacy fit-out."

"Excellent!" said Nat.

"You were right about me staying here to nail the job, weren't you? They're going to need me for a few nights because they're keeping the place open in the day and they don't want a whole team of guys hammering and wiring and making loads of noise during the day. So I won't be home tonight. Will you be OK by yourself?"

Nat saw a pattern emerging. "Just because we're back in England, doesn't mean you have to suddenly wrap me in cotton," he pointed out. "I stayed for two nights by myself in Barcelona when you did that kitchen shop and I was only twelve then!"

"OK, OK, I trust you. Anyway, I'll be back by mid-morning."

"I'll be gone to training by then," replied Nat.

"I'll be gone on Thursday night too, but back early on Friday morning. I'll see you then. But let's keep in regular contact, OK?"

"Definitely."

"Don't overdo it," cautioned his dad.

"I won't," sighed Nat.

When the coach got back to the Ivy Stadium, it was past 1 a.m. Nat caught a cab all the way back to the cottage. It cost forty pounds, but he could just about afford it.

It was 1:30 a.m. when he got home, and after cooking

himself some beans on toast he fell asleep almost immediately.

The next time he opened his eyes it was 8:37 a.m. He got out of bed and nearly fell over, so great was the strain in his legs. He steadied himself. If this was how he felt after a twenty-minute stint on the playing field, what would it be like if he ever got a full game?

The Times was lying on the doormat and Nat scooped it up and turned immediately to the back pages. On the inside was a match report on the Liverpool vs. Rangers game. Nat's eyes flew down the text until he spotted what he was looking for.

As a last throw of the dice, on seventy-six minutes, Fox brought on sixteen-year-old Nat Dixon, a recent acquisition whose paperwork has held him back from formally joining up with the squad. The teenager's presence was felt immediately with a couple of good passes.

But it was in the eighty-sixth minute that he revealed his precocious class. Deftly avoiding a full-on challenge from Ian Docherty (no mean feat), he swapped passes with Adilson and then played the Brazilian through with an audacious back heel. The Brazilian timed his run perfectly, smoothly ran past the goalkeeper's challenge and put the ball in the net.

However, in the third minute of added time, Dixon nearly canceled out his good work by felling Sutton right on the edge of the penalty area. The Liverpool players shouted for a penalty, but referee Neil Crossley decided Sutton had fallen outside the area, and awarded a free kick. Dixon was lucky to get away with a yellow card. Simic's powerful effort was pushed away by an agile dive from Chris Webb.

Dixon's reckless foul was a clear indication of his immaturity, but he's clearly a lad with talent and should be filed under "one to watch."

The rest of the report was a fair summation of the game, informing readers that Liverpool had enjoyed sixty-three percent of the possession and should have killed Rangers off early in the second half. Nat was just about to turn to the other match reports when his phone rang.

"Nat, it's Emi."

"Hi Emi."

"Bad news."

"What?"

"Fox has resigned."

Nat dropped his cereal spoon. "You're joking!"

"No. Kelvin just phoned me. It was on Sports Play FM. I'll see you later."

Nat grabbed the kitchen radio and turned to Sports Play FM. There was a discussion about England's next friendly international, followed by a phone-in about this year's British players at the Wimbledon Tennis Championships, but nothing about Fox. Nat gulped down the rest of his breakfast, got dressed, and hurried out of the cottage.

57

Clues

The atmosphere at Shelton Park was deadly. Even the usually cheerful Wildman looked down. Stan Evans showed up and called all of the players together.

"I know you've all heard by now that Sports Play FM have announced the boss's resignation, but I want you to keep your cool. It's completely unofficial and I've heard no word from him at all. If it is true, he'll have gone for a very good reason."

"But there's only one game left," pointed out Pierre Sacrois. "Why would he leave when he's gone this far with us?"

Evans shrugged his shoulders. "Football is a strange game," he replied, "and whatever the boss has done, we all need to support him."

The players exchanged glances and started muttering. Then Evans got the training session started and tried to inject some urgency into it. But the players' spirits were too low, and they trained with heavy hearts. Nat ran and passed and shot with dread coursing through him.

The locker room was almost silent after the session. People whispered as if they'd crashed in on a funeral. But then the door burst open and in walked Fox, a smile on his face, gum rotating like clockwork in his mouth.

Everyone rushed over to him, demanding to know what was going on.

"I know it was on the radio this morning that I resigned, but that's a hundred percent wrong!"

A massive cheer went up.

"I spoke to a journalist late last night who quoted me completely out of context. I said I might resign if we went down, and only then. He pushed me to say I'd go sooner because of Rangers' terrible league position but I stood my ground. Because I didn't oblige him with his story, he just made the thing up. I've spent the morning so far speaking to my lawyer to see if I can sue the guy."

"Go for it!" shouted the Wildman.

"There's no way you should resign, even if we do go down," insisted Emi. "If we get relegated it's our fault just as much as yours and we'll be right behind you, boss—fighting our way to come straight up again!"

Nat nodded along with the rest of the players, but he felt the heavy coil of knowledge wrapped around his neck. He was the only one who knew that the club would disappear if they went down.

Nat and Emi walked out together. "I'll give you a lift," said Emi.

"I'm OK, thanks, I'll get the bus."

"Are you sure?"

"I'm fine."

Nat left the locker room and took a shortcut toward the media suite. But as he approached the wooden door, he spied Steve Townsend inside through the glass panel. Townsend was deep in conversation with the tall, wiry guy Nat had seen him with in the narrow road near the Ivy Stadium. He was wearing the same blue pinstriped suit. They'd been having an argument then, but today their voices weren't raised.

Right! I'm going to find out what they're up to.

In a swift movement, he opened the door a fraction and slipped inside. Kneeling down behind a long banner that was tied to the lowest sections of a series of pillars, Nat crawled forward until he was in earshot of their conversation.

"I'm telling you," Townsend was saying. "We get in there and clean the place out."

"Yeah," agreed his friend, "they won't know what's hit them."

Nat held his breath to keep silent.

So Townsend is up to something seriously dodgy. It sounds like they're planning some kind of robbery. I'd love to know what it is.

But Townsend's conversation was over. He and the pinstripe guy hurried to a door on the far side of the room, and then they were gone.

*

At the offices of the *Sunday Crest* that night, Ray Swinton was working late. Because the Rangers line was that the Dixon kid had been spotted by Stan Evans, playing street soccer in the US, there was no one official to speak to. But this hadn't deterred Swinton. He was too long in the tooth to give up on a story when his instinct told him there might be something in it.

He'd spent hours on the phone, chasing up Stateside contacts from years ago. So far no one had provided him with anything concrete, just opinions, but the more he thought about it, the more he reckoned there was something fishy about Nat Dixon.

It was nudging 9:30 p.m. and he knew he should pack up and go straight home, see his wife, maybe eat something. But the potential of the story gnawed at him and as he looked at his list of contacts for what felt like the millionth time his desk phone rang. He picked it up before the first ring had finished.

"Is that Ray Swinton of the English *Sunday Crest* newspaper?" asked a heavily accented voice, maybe Spanish or Portuguese.

"Speaking."

"I have some information for you. Do you pay for stories?"

"We can," replied Swinton, grabbing a pen. "What have you got for me?"

For the next minute Swinton listened incredulously to the caller, scribbling down notes and feeling excitement in every nerve ending. This was the call he'd been waiting for.

"I want to talk about the money before I tell you anything else," said the caller.

"OK," said Swinton, "this is the way it works."

Fifteen minutes later, Swinton slammed down the phone triumphantly and immediately punched in the home number of his editor, Hugh Asquith.

"Hugh, it's Ray Swinton."

"Yes?" asked Asquith, somewhat irritably.

"I have the mother of all stories for you, something that will blow our rivals out of the water."

"I'm all ears, Ray," replied the editor, whose tone was now one of acute interest.

"I can't tell you what it is quite yet because there's one more person I need to speak to. But I need you to authorize some payments for a source."

"What? Without you explaining what the scoop is?" demanded Asquith.

"You've got to trust me on this one, Hugh. It's massive—I'm telling you. Release the funds and you'll get your story."

Asquith sighed. "This isn't the way I usually do things, Ray."

"I know, but you won't be disappointed. It will be front page, back page and at least four inside pages. It's huge! Just think of the envy of all of those other editors."

This was Asquith's Achilles heel and that was why Swinton had used it.

"OK," said Asquith. "I'll go with it. But if it crashes, you pay back the money."

"Fine," replied Swinton, "you have my word."

"I want it in writing," stated Asquith.

"Fine," agreed Swinton, "I'll sign on it. Now do I get the go-ahead?"

"How much do you need?"

58

Closing in

Dave was sitting on the back porch when Nat came down on Friday morning. They had spoken at least six times since the call on the coach coming back from Liverpool.

"Hello, stranger." Dave grinned. "I was wondering when you were going to show. Bagel? I got them on my way back from work."

"Yes, please. How's the job going?" asked Nat.

"Yeah, it's good." His dad nodded, handing him a bagel. "I'm pleased to be bringing in some cash now."

He studied Nat's face. "What's up?" he asked. "You look as if you've got something weighty on your mind."

Nat paused, deciding whether or not to tell him. "It's Ian Fox," said Nat.

"What about him?"

"Well, instead of being positive after the Liverpool game, he went crazy about my foul on Sutton. I didn't really want to tell you over the phone, but it's been driving me a bit nuts."

Dave pulled a face. "That's a shame. He should have praised you for the killer pass, but…"

"But what?"

Dave sighed. "It *was* a bit of a wild challenge, wasn't it? They showed it on TV. It wasn't really necessary."

"What? You agree with him?" exploded Nat.

"Hang on!" said his dad. "I'm not saying I agree with him, I just think there's a lot to be learned from that incident."

"What would you know?" yelled Nat.

"Nat, calm down!" shouted his dad.

"I will NOT calm down! I'm the one who's playing professional football now, not YOU! So I don't need your opinions!"

Nat turned and stormed back into the house, grabbed his bag and started heading toward the front door. Dave ran in after him.

"Come on, Nat!" called Dave. "There's no need to be so sensitive. You have to be able to handle criticism along with praise."

But Nat was already outside. He slammed the front door behind him and stomped down the track.

Nat was in a bad mood throughout training. He couldn't concentrate, but he was acutely aware of Fox's eyes on him and didn't want to blow his chances of making an appearance in the next game—the big one—the last game of the season, home to Man United. But he kept on thinking about Fox's dressing-down and his dad's agreement with Fox. It enraged him that the two men could be so unfair. He could take criticism like anyone else; he just wanted it to be balanced with positive comments.

Emi asked if he wanted to crash at his place for the night. Nat gratefully accepted the offer, but said he wanted to spend a bit of time alone after training to clear his head.

He had made it past the Shelton Park security gate

and was preparing to go for a long walk, to sort out his thoughts, when he spied someone standing in his path. He recognized him from the byline photo that always appeared above his pieces in the *Sunday Crest*: Ray Swinton, the world's number-one expert on all Rangers matters. Swinton was one person he really didn't want to see, but it would look a bit stupid—not to mention suspicious—to run away.

"Nat? Can I have a word?" Swinton called out, hurrying toward him.

Nat put his hands in his pockets. "What do you want?" he asked defensively.

"I just wanted to have a chat about your impressive arrival on the scene," said the journalist. "You know, get a feel of what it's been like to be dropped in at the deep end."

"OK," Nat said reluctantly, "but I've only got a few minutes."

"That's fine." Swinton nodded, quickly switching on a mini voice recorder and holding it up between them.

"Do you have to use that?" Nat frowned.

"Forget about it," replied Swinton. "It's just for the record."

"OK," conceded Nat.

"I'd like to begin with what it feels like to pull on the Rangers shirt and turn out at a place like Anfield."

"It feels … great," said Nat guardedly. "I've always wanted to play for Rangers, ever since I was … a little kid."

"A dream-come-true sort of thing?"

"Sure. Players like Neil Duffy and Paolo Corragio are heroes of mine."

"Must be weird playing alongside them."

"Very weird ... but great."

"What was it like making that assist for Adilson's goal in the Liverpool game? You did intend it, didn't you?"

"I did." Nat nodded. "But there was a bit of luck involved too. Sometimes those kinds of passes are duds."

"What about you bursting onto the scene? It's all been a bit sudden, hasn't it? It's as if you dropped into Rangers from the heavens."

"What do you mean?" asked Nat warily.

"Come on, Nat," said Swinton. "Everyone else might believe the story about Stan Evans spotting you in a game of street soccer in the United States, but I don't. You were registered with the Association in the January transfer window, but your paperwork was only sorted out in the last few weeks? That's a new one to me."

"Er ... I..."

"What about the fact that you're not sixteen?"

Nat felt as if someone had just grabbed him by the neck and squeezed the very life out of him.

"You're not sixteen, are you, Nat? Come on, I know your secret. You're only thirteen!"

"Of course I'm sixteen!" cried Nat shakily, "I don't know what you're talking about. It's absolute rubbish!"

"That's not what my contact in Rio de Janeiro told me last night."

Nat froze.

"You did spend a year in Rio, didn't you?" Swinton probed further.

Nat said nothing. He was far too flustered to manage even a denial.

"I've been a journalist for thirty-five years, Nat," said Swinton, "and I know an explosive story when I see one. It all makes complete sense. Ian Fox is desperate. He or Stan Evans see you playing somewhere, find out you're only thirteen, but in desperation ask you to join up. That's it, isn't it?"

"That's … that's not it," replied Nat hoarsely.

"My contact in Brazil is a hundred percent convinced it's you, and he has plenty of info to share about your time in Brazil. So I'm going to run with the story, not this Sunday, but the Sunday after. The Premier League season will be over and this will be the only story in town. It's going to be huge. It's up to you now, whether you want to admit the truth and get your side of the story in the paper, or whether you're going to deny it and be fully exposed. Which is it to be?"

Thoughts cascaded into Nat's panicked mind.

Who is Swinton's contact in Brazil? How on earth did he manage to find them?

But then suddenly his mind was freed from the mess as a clear idea floated into place.

"There's another way of doing this," said Nat, suddenly thinking about Steve Townsend's conversation with the pinstripe-suit guy.

"Let's get in there and clean them out."

"Yes?" asked Swinton.

"I do deny your story absolutely—it's garbage, but I know you journalists often publish lies and don't worry about the consequences."

"That's your opinion and you're entitled to it."

"What if I told you I had a true story; something that's far, far better than your fabricated one?"

"What kind of story?"

"It's massive."

"You're bluffing, aren't you, to put me off the scent?"

"I swear I'm not. Look, Mr. Swinton…"

"Call me Ray."

"Look, Ray. I promise you I'll get you something, something really huge. But you've got to give me a little bit of time to get everything ready before I tell you."

Swinton chewed this over for a few seconds.

"I still think you're bluffing, but…" Swinton paused.

Nat eyed him anxiously.

"I'll tell you what," said Swinton. "Like I told you, I'm not going to run the story until next Sunday. I want a good clear week to trail it in the paper."

"So?"

"So I'll give you until the end of the Man United game this Sunday. If you don't come up with the goods by 5 p.m. I'm running with my original story next Sunday."

Nat breathed a sigh of relief—even if he'd only managed to squeeze some more time out of Swinton, it was better than nothing. The only problem was, he had to get a juicier story and his only lead was Townsend. Townsend was definitely up to something. But what was it? And what if it wasn't some kind of crime?

I have to stop Swinton going with the thirteen-year-old story. Should I tell Stan Evans and Ian Fox about all of this? No, I'll try to deal with it myself, and if that fails I'll bring them in on it.

"Do we have a deal?" asked Swinton, reaching out his hand to shake Nat's.

Nat kept his hands by his side. "We have a deal," he replied.

59

What Comes Home?

Several hours and multiple computer games later, Nat and Emi were sitting in the small yard at the back of Emi's place. They were perched on red-and-white striped deckchairs on the patio, looking out at the two neat lines of shrubs that framed the perfectly mown grass. Mrs. Felgate had made them shepherd's pie and they were now sipping from two bottles of Coke.

"So what do you think about Sunday?" asked Emi. "Do you think we can beat Man United?"

Nat grimaced. "On paper, after our form and their form this season, they should … kill us!"

Emi laughed. "My thoughts exactly, but on the day, anything's possible. We've got some great players … and a couple of lousy ones."

"You couldn't mean Mr. Townsend, could you?"

Emi nodded. "Steve Townsend is an impediment to the team. It's as though we're all pulling in one direction and he's pulling in another. That man is so full of negative vibes."

"Totally," agreed Nat, "but he's part of the furniture, isn't he? He and the gaffer go back years, don't they?"

"That's the problem," replied Emi taking a swig of his drink. "They've known each other forever, but it's not like they're friends or anything."

"Do you think Steve Townsend could be … could be involved in something criminal?" asked Nat casually.

Emi turned around to face him. "Criminal? How do you mean?"

"I don't know, he just seems kind of shady."

"He's definitely shady!" Emi laughed. "But I don't know if he's a criminal. Have you got any evidence?"

"Nah," Nat replied, "nothing specific, it's just a hunch."

"Cool," said Emi, "for a minute there I thought you were heading into TV cop drama territory!"

Nat suddenly felt completely drained. There was so much new and weird stuff going on, it felt as if he were carrying a sack of concrete slabs on his shoulders. Wouldn't it be a relief to share all of this with someone—the truth about his age, Swinton, Townsend, everything? And Emi would be the best person to tell. He was a top guy—a good listener, sympathetic.

"What's on your mind, Nat?" asked Emi.

Nat pursed his lips. "Nothing," he replied, "I'm cool."

Nat stayed at Emi's that night. He checked his phone for messages before he went to bed. His dad had left two, both saying he was sorry for yelling at Nat and that he didn't want there to be a *broigus* between them, that his performance against Liverpool had been excellent and even though he fouled Sutton it wasn't the end of the world, and he was on a giant learning curve. Nat smiled when he'd finished listening. He would phone his dad in the morning and offer his own apology. And even though he hated to admit it, his dad and Fox were right. He could have cost Rangers the

Liverpool game. He had dived in without thinking. Well, he was making big life adjustments every day. He wasn't playing games in the park any more—this was the big time and he needed to get used to it.

*

Tanner was watching a boxing match on cable when his phone rang.

"It's Knight."

Tanner sat up. "Where the blazes have you been? It's been a week since the police raid and I've heard nothing from you. I've pulled out a lot of stops for this project and I don't appreciate being cut loose."

"I wasn't cutting you loose," replied Knight in a calm, persuasive voice. "I was making sure that everything was smoothed over."

"Meaning what?"

"The police raid was concerned with just one of our investors. It was connected to his arms-dealing income stream. It was him the police were after. They know absolutely nothing about our little operation. That particular investor is lying low and has pulled out of the venture."

"What about the other three?"

"They took a bit of persuasion, but eventually I managed to convince them that we're in the clear."

"So they're still on board?"

"Very much so; the wheels have been put in motion. The money's placed. Everything's going according to plan."

"So we're on?" asked Tanner.

"Absolutely," replied Knight. "We're on."

60

On the Case

Mid-afternoon the following day, Nat walked into the gym at the Ivy Stadium. He'd slept until noon at Emi's. They had played *Danger Force 11* for a couple of hours and then grabbed something to eat. When Nat had said he was going to the gym, Emi had declined the offer to join him; he wanted to listen to some music he'd just downloaded.

Nat headed straight for the weights. If Stan Evans wanted a beefier Nat, then he would deliver one.

Nat moved from the weights, did twenty minutes on the cycling machine and then twenty on the treadmill. He thought about his relationship with his dad. Things between them had been more tempestuous in the last few days than they had been in the previous seven years! First the wretched disappointment over the cottage, then Ian Fox's offer and now a blow-out about the rights and wrongs of Nat's actions in the Liverpool game. This wasn't exactly the usual fare on the plate of a thirteen-year-old!

After twenty minutes on the rowing machine and a long warm-down, Nat went into the steam room and lay down. Then he showered, changed, and phoned the cottage.

"Nat?" said Dave. "Where are you?"

"I'm at the club. I've just done a session in the gym."

"Look, Nat," said his dad, "like I said on my messages,

I'm sorry about criticizing you; I didn't mean to. You've been thrown into this *meshuggah* situation and you did what you thought was best. I'm not condoning it, but I've reminded myself that you're only thirteen and that this whole thing at times might be too overwhelming for you to handle…"

"I'm sorry too, Dad," Nat cut in. "I was out of line to scream at you. I got ahead of myself, played the big shot."

"No, you didn't," countered Dave. "You just said what you felt. I might be your dad, but you're the one in there at a professional club. I've never been in that position."

"I know, Dad, but that doesn't give me the right to mouth off."

There was a pause on the line.

"Are we both finished apologizing?" asked Dave.

Nat laughed. "I guess so. What are you doing today?"

"I'm going to do some work on the back field, then pop into Lowerbury to get a few bits and pieces. Do you need anything?"

"Nah, I'm fine."

"Are you coming home tonight?"

"I'm not sure. I might stay at Emi's. I'll decide later and let you know."

"Sounds fine by me."

"Great."

"And, Nat?"

"Yeah?"

"Thanks for calling."

"No problem."

Nat left the locker room and spied none other than Steve Townsend hurrying away beside the pinstripe guy.

I have to know what they're up to.

Nat waited until they were out of sight and then dashed after them. He flung open the door they'd gone through and scanned the hallway. There was no sign of them. They couldn't have gone far. He raced down the corridor, past some meeting rooms and then down the stairs into the lobby.

They weren't there. Nat clenched his fists and ran toward the revolving doors. He hurried outside the stadium. Again no sign. He could have hit himself with frustration.

He backtracked into the stadium and was running down another corridor when through a window he spied a silver Porsche pulling out of the parking lot.

Townsend's car!

Nat flew down some stairs and back through the revolving doors that led to the street. He spied the Porsche just pulling onto the road.

To his utter joy, a cab was driving down the street with its light on. Nat frantically waved it down. It pulled over and the cabbie wound down his window. "Where to, buddy?" he asked.

"I know it sounds stupid," Nat blurted out, "but could you follow that Porsche?"

61

Follow Through

The driver looked down the road at the silver vehicle and raised his arms in the air. "If you want to follow it and you've got enough money to pay me to follow it, I'll do it."

"Thanks!" said Nat, jumping into the back of the cab and slamming the door behind him.

As the driver pulled away and stepped on the gas, Nat's brain was racing. OK, he was following Townsend, but to where? Were they about to do the job now? Would he be able to watch them doing it? Would he then call the police? Should he phone Ray Swinton and meet up with him at the scene of the crime?

The Porsche cut down a number of side streets and then started heading out west. The busy roads soon gave way to fields and quieter streets. Luckily the cabbie was an excellent driver and always managed to stay a couple of cars behind the Porsche to remain unseen, but near enough to keep the other vehicle in his sights.

Finally the Porsche slowed down and turned onto a rutted single-track road. The cabbie waited until it had turned a corner and edged out of sight before he followed it. The Porsche had a good thirty-second head start, and when the cab nosed around the corner, Nat saw it up ahead, parked outside a large and remote farmhouse.

There was no one outside. Townsend must already be inside the building.

Nat pulled out his wallet.

"I know it's none of my business," said the cabbie, "but what's so special about the Porsche and its driver that makes you want to follow it?"

Nat handed him some cash and opened the cab door. "I'm not sure," he said. "It's just something I've got to do."

"Suit yourself." The driver shrugged, taking the money and slipping it into his jacket pocket.

Nat got out of the cab. He shut the door as quietly as he could. The driver nodded at him and started reversing back up the track. Slowly, Nat walked forward, looking at the overgrown grass and weeds at the side of the track and searching the farmhouse for any sign of movement.

The house was whitewashed and had a thatched roof. There was a yard at the front where the Porsche was parked, and a couple of potted plants on either side of the front door.

Nat crouched down and hurried around the side of the building. There was no noise coming from within, but Nat was sure that Townsend was inside. Somehow he had to find out what Townsend was up to. He could only hope it was something really dramatic. It was the only way he was going to get Ray Swinton off his back.

Nat went further along the side of the house and then spotted an open window beside an oak door. He eased forward and heard two muffled voices coming from inside.

He placed his ear against the oak door. Unfortunately, at that moment the door was yanked open and Nat fell straight inside.

He looked up and came face-to-face with ... Chris Webb.

"Nat," snapped Webb, "what are you doing here?"

Nat stood up and stared at the Rangers goalie in shock. What was *Webb* doing here? Surely he wasn't involved in Townsend's criminal plan? The two of them hated each other, didn't they?

"I followed you, I mean ... I..." Nat's sentence trailed off into the air.

"What is it?" demanded a gruff voice. A tough-looking guy with black eyes, a crew cut, and a scar on his left cheek barged down the hallway and scowled at Nat.

"You!" he snarled. "The new kid on the block. What do you think you're doing?"

Webb stamped his foot on the floor. "You stupid idiot!" he shouted at Nat. "Why did you have to come here?"

"I'll go," Nat replied, raising his hands in the air in a gesture of innocence.

"Forget it," hissed the rough guy, grabbing Nat by the jacket collar and dragging him inside. Webb followed and slammed the oak door behind them. They walked down a narrow hall and then emerged in the farmhouse's kitchen. It was pretty sparse, with a sink and a round table flanked by three chairs. It didn't look as if anyone lived here.

Nat sensed an opportunity to explain himself and get away from Webb and his scary friend.

"Look, me being here is nothing to do with you, Chris," he began. "I was following … or at least thought I was following Steve Townsend."

Webb slapped his forehead with the palm of his right hand. "The Porsche—of course!"

Nat looked blank.

"My friend here, Mr. Tanner, just bought the exact same model and color as Townsend's. Why were you following him, anyway?"

Nat paused for a second, not sure whether or not to divulge his reason. In the end he opted to spill the beans. Maybe being honest would get him out of here.

"I thought he was involved in some kind of robbery," explained Nat.

"Why would you think that?" demanded Webb.

"I overheard him saying something about cleaning the place out."

Webb let out a cold, false laugh. "Steve Townsend isn't capable of managing a bank account, so I think a robbery would be well beyond him!"

"So what did he mean?"

"Was he with a tall, wiry, ugly guy?" asked Webb.

The pinstripe guy! "Yes." Nat nodded.

"That's Frank Driver, his long-time gambling buddy. They're a couple of losers who have been planning for weeks to make a killing at one of the casinos in town. They must have been talking about that."

"So there's no big theft going on?" asked Nat.

"No chance!" replied Webb.

Nat's face dropped. So he'd got the Townsend thing wrong, and his massive story for Swinton had just died. But what was Webb doing here?

"It's too risky to let him go," said Tanner quietly. "He's seen us together."

Webb nodded. "Chuck him in the storeroom and we'll think about what to do."

"Hang on a sec," protested Nat, shrinking back. "I promise I won't say anything about this to anyone. I've already forgotten your friend's name, Chris, and I won't be able to describe him."

"Nice try!" barked Tanner. "Now empty your pockets."

"Forget it," answered Nat defiantly.

No sooner had he said this, than Tanner lunged forward and yanked Nat's arms behind his back.

Nat yelled in pain and struggled ferociously, twisting his body and lashing out at Tanner with his legs. But Tanner was incredibly strong and Nat was no match for him.

"Do it!" yelled Tanner.

Chris Webb quickly checked Nat's jacket and found his cell phone.

"Smash it!" ordered Tanner.

Webb dropped the phone on the floor and stamped on it several times until it was lying in pieces across the floor. He picked up the SIM card and pocketed it.

Then Webb checked Nat's pants pockets and discovered his wallet and his keys. He chucked them onto a table.

"Right," said Tanner, dragging Nat across the room, "it's time to get you out of sight."

"Where are you taking me?" shouted Nat, struggling again with every ounce of energy in his body. But once again, Tanner's grip tightened and Nat had no chance of breaking free. Tanner stopped when they came to a steel door and kicked it open.

"I strongly suggest you keep your mouth shut!" ordered Tanner, shoving Nat forward and slamming the door behind him. Nat listened to the sound of bolts being shut and a key being turned.

62

Lock-in

Nat banged on the door with his fists. "LET ME OUT!" he demanded, but all he could hear was the muffled sound of footsteps walking away.

Nat turned around and stared at his prison in the light offered by one tiny and high window. It was barred. The space was cold and dank and smelled of mildew. There was nothing in the room, save for what looked like an old cleaning cart with a broken dustpan and brush, a moldy cloth and a couple of cleaning products that looked years past their sell-by date.

Nat groaned. How could he have been so wrong about Townsend's plans and got caught up in this Webb–Tanner thing instead? If they'd locked him in this storeroom they were obviously up to something serious, but what?

And there was something else bothering him; he'd told both his dad and Emi that he might stay at the other's place and that he'd let them know later. If he didn't phone them, they'd just assume he wasn't staying with them. If he was kept here tonight, they wouldn't know to sound the alarm when he didn't show up.

He started pacing around the room, going over everything in his head. Was Webb involved in some kind of unscrupulous property deal involving this junk-heap farmhouse? Was Webb some kind of criminal realtor or something?

After walking around the room for what seemed like hours, Nat banged on the door.

"I'M THIRSTY!" he shouted. "I NEED A DRINK!"

There was no response from outside. Nat tried to control the panic snaking up inside him. Maybe Webb and Tanner just had to complete a task or something that they didn't want him to see and then they'd let him go?

Could I jump one of them if they came into the storeroom?

Unlikely. Nat was well built for his age, but he was still a kid. Both Webb and Tanner were giants by comparison and he wouldn't stand a chance. And there was absolutely no other way out of here. The window was too high, too small and barred. The only exit point was the door.

He slammed his fist into the door. "CHRIS!" he yelled. "I NEED A DRINK!"

The silence that met his request was chilling.

Nat slumped onto the floor. He took off his jacket and rolled it up to make a pillow. He lay back on it and gazed at the darkness of the storeroom ceiling. How long were they going to keep him in here? It was the Rangers vs. Man United game tomorrow—surely he and Webb weren't going to miss it?

He drifted off into a shallow and uncomfortable sleep but woke up when he heard the bolt sliding back and the key twisting. Pretending to still be asleep, he turned to face away from the door, made soft snoring sounds and kept his eyes tightly shut.

Webb walked toward him and leaned over his body. "He's

flat out," Webb announced to Tanner, who was standing in the doorway.

"Good," replied Tanner. "It's a pain that he showed up, but nothing is untreatable."

"Fine," said Webb walking back across the room.

The two of them stood in the doorway talking.

"Have you ever thrown a game before?" asked Tanner.

As soon as the words were out of Tanner's mouth, Nat's eyes opened.

"Nah," replied Webb. "Not that I haven't been asked, of course. But this offer was in a different class. This is retire-on-an-Antiguan-beach territory, and only a complete idiot would say no to it."

Nat's body was rigid with shock. Chris Webb, the man who had Hatton Rangers' lifeblood in his veins, Mr. Loyalty, was going to let Man United win because he'd been offered a huge amount of money? He was going to get Rangers relegated! Nat knew this kind of stuff sometimes happened—but in the Premier League, over such a vital game?

Nat recalled all of the contact he'd had with Chris Webb in his short time at the club. All those smiles and pats on the back were just showpieces—lies to convince everyone that he was devoted to Rangers, while plotting the club's downfall behind their backs.

"Do you know how big the pot is?" Webb asked Tanner.

"Don't worry about the money," snapped Tanner. "Just do your bit on the field and the cash will come rolling in."

"Agreed," said Webb. "Let's get out of here. We'll come back and check on him later."

At that point, something in Nat snapped. He was seething at Webb's plan to sink Rangers. Before he could control himself, he was up on his feet, charging toward them. A tiny part of him thought he might be able to barge past them and make an escape, but Tanner was more than ready for him. In one swift move, he stepped to the side. Nat went surging onward and Tanner was perfectly positioned to grab Nat's right arm and slam it behind his back.

"LET GO OF ME!" yelled Nat.

The next second he felt a cracking pain on the back of his head and then everything went black.

63

No Escape

Nat woke up and instantly felt a searing pain at the back of his head where he'd been hit. His whole body ached, his throat felt like an arid valley, and his stomach was taut with hunger. He lifted his head a fraction and winced in agony.

Memories of the night before slowly tipped into his brain like sludge: following the Porsche, sneaking round the side of the farmhouse, finding Chris Webb and Tanner, hearing the match-fixing plan. It was impossible to believe: Chris Webb, Rangers' most loyal servant and backbone of the club, was planning to cost the club its Premiership status to line his pockets with a golden payday. How could he do it? The guy was complete and utter scum.

Slowly, Nat got to his feet, checking his body for bone breakages and feeling a sliver of relief that there were none.

If only they hadn't smashed my phone!

He walked over to the storeroom door and put his ear against it. Nothing. He tried the door handle. He shoulder-barged the door. He kicked it. But none of the actions achieved anything. The door was well secured.

Today had promised to be one of the most exciting days in his life, but it had turned into a total nightmare. Nat smashed his fists against the door in anger and frustration. What were Webb and Tanner up to at this minute? And what were they planning on doing with him?

9:10 A.M.

Dave sank another cup of coffee and put the cup into the sink. He was pleased Nat had become friends with Emi and Kelvin so quickly. They were both excellent lads, not to mention players with very big futures ahead of them. He was also delighted that Emi was so hospitable—letting Nat stay over at his place. It was one less thing for him to worry about and meant Nat could be much nearer the stadium. They'd probably stayed up late last night, playing computer games or plotting Man United's downfall.

Dave checked his watch. It was far too early for Nat to be up; if there wasn't such a vital game today, he'd probably stay in bed all day. Dave grabbed the first of the kitchen shelves he'd made and got to work. He'd try Nat's phone later.

9:55 A.M.

"HELLO! IS ANYBODY THERE?"

Nat beat his fists against the door, the panic threatening to engulf him. What if Webb and Tanner were planning just to leave him here? How long would he last without food and water? A week? Ten days?

"HELLO!"

He hit the door another couple of times and then walked away from it.

I've got to get a grip.

But as Nat started to pace round the storeroom, the same thoughts kept flooding his head.

There are two of them and only one of me. Tanner is a complete thug, who clearly relishes violence. There are no hiding places in here. I have nothing to arm myself with. They have the keys—I have nothing.

It was a situation that didn't look good from any angle.

64

Worlds Apart

10:08 A.M.

Steve Townsend rolled out of bed and stood on an empty beer can. He yelped and kicked the can, which flew across the room and knocked a row of books off a shelf. He cursed at the heaviness of his losses at the casino last night. When he'd begged for more credit at the end of the evening, he'd been escorted off the premises. Far from cleaning the place out, the place had cleaned him out. And that included all of the Porsche money. How could he have blown so much cash in one night?

He gritted his teeth and stumbled to the bathroom. The only thing that had gotten him out of bed was the thought of that Dixon kid trying to oust him from the team. Well, he'd show Dixon who the man was this afternoon. He'd defeat Man United by himself if he had to.

10:36 A.M.

The pain at the back of Nat's head was still there, but it wasn't as ferocious as it had been when he woke up.

He was sitting cross-legged on the floor of the storeroom, conserving energy. In the last hour his spirits had risen and sunk more times than he could count. In his

258

positive moments, he imagined the police getting wind of the plan, smashing down the storeroom door and driving him straight to the stadium in a siren-blaring car.

But in his negative moments, he couldn't see beyond the walls of this crummy prison. Webb would throw the game, Rangers would be relegated, and he would be at the mercy of that psychopath Tanner. It was an ugly scenario and as the seconds ticked by, Nat felt that some kind of endgame was edging ever closer.

10:58 A.M.

Dave studied the first two shelves he'd put up and nodded. He was often so involved with carpentry jobs that he never did things like put up shelves in his own place. But this was different. They were going to be living here for a long time and now was the time to start putting down foundations. He reached for his phone and dialed Nat's number. It went straight to voicemail.

"Hi Nat, it's Dad. I hope you and Emi are up, or at least are going to get up pretty soon. Apparently there's an important football match today, something to do with a team called HATTON RANGERS! Wouldn't want the two of you to *shluff* through the match—I think that might get you into a bit of trouble with Ian Fox! Anyway, give me a quick call when you're up and ready and I'll see you at the stadium."

Dave hung up and shoved the phone in his pocket. He didn't see that it was almost out of power.

65

Communication Breakdown

11:46 A.M.

Adilson was the first Rangers player to get to the stadium. He needed a rub-down on his sore back and liked to spend ages before a match getting showered, running over all of his moves in his head, and going through his intricate pre-match rituals (which included trying out five identical pairs of cleats and selecting the ones that felt "right" for the game). He had to play brilliantly today. Half of Brazil would be watching him and urging him on, while the other half would be roaring for Man United. It was the biggest game of his career—no question.

12:15 P.M.

Nat lay on the floor with his head resting on his rolled-up jacket. He kept drifting into sleep and dreaming he was back on Copa Cabana beach, playing in one of the massive games, twisting and shimmying and trying to score ever more outrageous goals. In his waking moments, he remembered where he was and tried to raise his spirits, but the fight was slowly draining out of him.

He thought of his dad. He'd be leaving for the game soon, all fired up and excited about the prospect of seeing his son turn out for the team again, even if it was only for five minutes at the end of a 5–0 drubbing at the hands of Manchester United. Nat knew he should try to stay awake, but the exhaustion pulled on his eyelids, and he fell under its spell once again.

12:54 P.M.

Stan Evans pushed open the door and scanned the home-team locker room.

"Has anyone seen Webby or Nat Dixon?" he shouted.

Adilson trapped the ball he was juggling with, turned around, and shrugged his shoulders. Paolo Corragio shook his head.

"Have you seen Nat?" Evans called across to Emi, who'd just stepped out of the shower.

"No," answered Emi. "He stayed with his dad last night. Why?"

"It doesn't matter." Stan tutted, turning and heading out the door.

He walked down the hall, concern pinching his face. He'd worked with Chris Webb for years and the guy had never been this late on a match day. The man was a model professional. He was usually one of the first in.

He went through all of his pre-match preparations and then spent time with reserve goalkeeper Graham Dalston. There were just under two hours until kick-off and Webb hadn't shown up.

And where was Nat? Surely he hadn't started taking

liberties with his timekeeping? Stan shook his head. Something was up; he could feel it in his gut. And his gut was very rarely wrong.

1:11 P.M.

In the press box, Ray Swinton finished a conversation with a guy from a French newspaper who was doing a feature on French players in the Premier League. He looked down at the groundsmen digging their little pitchforks into sections of the turf. It was the last day of the season, and they'd kept the field in excellent condition over the last nine months.

Swinton took a sip from his bottle of water and looked around the soccer ground. He was pretty sure that Nat Dixon's stuff about getting a better story was nothing more than bluster, a kid's way of trying to buy more time. Maybe he'd been stupid in giving Dixon until the end of the game today to come up with the goods. There was no alternative story.

No, as soon as the game was finished he'd file his match report and then pay a visit to Asquith and reveal the scoop. Asquith was bound to go wild over it. A thirteen-year-old kid playing in the Premier League! This was top-drawer material. As well as giving the *Sunday Crest* a massive circulation boost, it would also increase Swinton's national and international reputation. He imagined correspondents from across the globe battling to talk to the man who broke this incredible story.

The Net Tightens

1:26 P.M.

Ian Fox was completely freaking out.

He was locked in his office with Stan Evans. They'd been on the phone for the last half-hour trying every known contact of Chris Webb's and redialing Nat's dad, without any luck. Evans had handed out a large batch of complimentary tickets—in various parts of the stadium— for today's game, and had no record of which tickets he'd given to whom. It would just take too long to try and find out where Dave was sitting.

"WHAT ON EARTH ARE WE GOING TO DO?" shouted Fox. "Without Webby we'll ship in goals, and we may well need Nat today! But NEITHER OF THEM IS ANYWHERE! This can't be happening!"

"I don't know what to say," said Evans, wiping the sweat off his forehead. "We've tried everyone. Do you think they're together?"

"Why would they be together?" Fox sighed. "They hardly know each other. It's just got to be a coincidence, but a pretty bad coincidence to happen on the most important day of our careers. I could kill them!"

"Maybe something's happened to them," Evans suggested.

"Like what?" replied Fox. "If Webb got knocked down by a car, there would be a scramble to get his autograph. People around here know who he is. I just don't get it."

They stood in silence, lost in their own thoughts.

"This is bad news," said Evans finally.

"Tell me about it," grimaced Fox.

2:07 P.M.

Nat woke up as the storeroom door was unlocked and opened. He stood up quickly and watched as Webb and Tanner entered. Tanner wore his default icy expression.

"Look, guys," said Nat, holding up his hands. "I don't care what you're up to. That's your business. It's nothing to do with me. Just let me go and I won't say anything about this whole experience to anyone."

"Are you joking?" snapped Tanner, clenching his fists.

"No," replied Nat quickly, "I'm serious. I'll go and that's the last you'll hear from me."

Webb laughed, a short, fake laugh. "Do you think we're idiots?" he cried. "Do you really think we'd let you out to go and blab to the rest of the world about being locked up by the Hatton Rangers goalie and about things you might or might not have heard?"

"I'll say nothing," said Nat, trying to stop his voice from sounding too desperate.

Webb ignored him and turned to Tanner. "Hit me in the face, Tanner. Make it look like I was involved in a struggle."

A sly smile flitted across Tanner's lips.

The guy clearly loves violence.

Tanner pulled his fist back and smashed it straight into Webb's face. Webb shouted in pain and staggered backward.

"You didn't have to make it that hard!" he snarled as he steadied himself.

The effect was instant. His lip was swollen and bleeding. His cheek and eye socket were already black and would be a nice hue of bluey-purple before long. "You want to make it realistic or not?" snapped Tanner. "It won't stop you from playing."

"OK," Webb agreed. "I need to make it to the stadium. I have a tale to spin and then I have to get moving. By 4:45 we'll be extremely rich."

"That's the plan," said Tanner quietly.

"Dixon knows too much," said Webb.

A shiver of terror slithered up Nat's spine. "What are you going to do?" he shouted in desperation, running toward the door.

Tanner blocked his way and shoved him backward. He hurried out of the room, while Webb kept watch over Nat. A few moments later, Tanner returned, carrying a sleek silver case.

"I'd better be off," said Webb, shooting a nervous glance at Tanner. "Are you sure there's no other way to do this?"

Tanner shook his head firmly. "I told you, I'll deal with it. Now go!"

Webb swallowed, gave Nat a quick look and hurried out of the room.

When his footsteps had died away, Tanner opened the case and pulled out a gun.

No Clues

2:17 P.M.

Fox, Evans, and the rest of the team sat in the locker room in funereal silence, well aware that in about fifteen minutes they'd need to go out onto the field, welcome the fans, and warm up. But they were all shocked by the no-show by their goalie and their latest teen acquisition. No one had any idea where either of them was, and this was more than deeply troubling: it had disaster written all over it.

2:20 P.M.

Dave took his seat in the Ivy Stadium and rubbed his hands together. Half of him felt nervous and full of fear. Man United were an incredible team. They'd dropped very few points this season and they were the favorites by miles to win this game. But the other part of him felt optimistic—anything could happen in a football match. Sometimes the underdogs came through. Maybe Rangers could win this.

In about two and a quarter hours he would know Rangers' fate. With luck, they'd get the right result and maybe, just maybe, his son would get to play a part.

He pulled out his phone to try Nat again in an attempt to get in a quick pre-match chat, but noticed with frustration that it was out of power. He cursed himself for not checking and charging it earlier.

2:35 P.M.

The crowd roared as the Rangers players ran onto the field. The players clapped to all four sides of the stadium and began passing the ball around, shooting into the practice net and doing short, powerful running exercises. The Man United players came out to cheers from their traveling supporters and boos from the Rangers fans.

In the press box, Ray Swinton made a face. What was Graham Dalston doing in the Rangers goal? Where was Chris Webb? He also noticed that Nat Dixon was absent. Where was the kid? Could his absence be anything to do with the incredible scoop he'd promised Swinton? Surely not? The kid was bluffing … wasn't he?

After ten minutes both teams retreated back into the stadium. The United players were totally focused on the game. The Rangers players were thinking about their absent teammates and trying to figure out what had happened to them.

68

The Full Horror

Ian Fox was about to send his players back out onto the field when the changing-room door was flung open and Chris Webb burst in. There was a gasp of shock at his appearance. His lip was hugely swollen, his cheek was covered with a huge bruise, he had a severe black eye, and his skin was so pale he looked as if he'd spent the last few months in a Siberian jail.

"What on earth happened to you?" cried Fox, getting to his feet and striding over to his goalkeeper.

The players were sitting in a horseshoe of benches. Every one of them stared at Webb, stunned by his dramatic entrance. Fox and Evans were equally shocked.

Webb gulped several times and leaned against the wall.

When he spoke, his voice was hoarse and shaky.

"I was with Nat," he began. "We'd both been working out in the gym. I said I'd give him a lift home. But they were waiting for us in the parking lot."

"Who were?" demanded Fox.

Webb grimaced as if he'd just been punched in the solar plexus.

"It was four guys, maybe five," he said, closing his eyes

for a moment as if the memory was unbearable, and then opening them again. "They were wearing balaclavas."

He shivered.

"What happened?" asked Fox.

"They … they … chucked us into the back of a white van. They tied us up and covered our faces and mouths. We struggled like crazy. I could hear Nat screaming like a wild animal. But … we … we had no chance."

He took a shaky breath as everyone in the room tried to take in this shocking news.

"We drove … for ages … and then…"

Tears started flooding down Webb's cheeks.

Fox put a hand on his shoulder. "Go on, Chris," he said quietly, "we're all with you."

Webb wiped the tears off his cheeks with the back of his hand and took a sip of water from a bottle that Adilson handed him.

"We drove for about an hour," Webb went on, "and they locked us in a room for ages without untying our hands or uncovering our faces. I … I … was scared— seriously scared."

Fox gripped Webb's shoulder in support.

"Finally they came back and told us their plan. They were going to ask Rangers for a huge sum to release both of us. They'd only meant to grab me. Nat just happened to be in the wrong place at the wrong time. I'm…" Webb broke down, his body shaking violently. It took him several seconds to regain his composure. "I worked for ages on my hand ties and finally managed to get them off. I ripped the tape off my mouth and set Nat free. We listened at the door but heard nothing."

Every single person in the room was staring at him with intense concentration.

"We waited for ages and eventually two of them showed up. I was so fired up that I floored both of them. We opened a window, climbed across a flat roof, and shimmied down a drainpipe. Nat was … he was … doing great. In the distance we could see a major road and we ran toward it. We'd only got about fifty yards when there was a shout behind us. It was them. We kept running and a second later I heard a crack and something whistled past us. It was … a bullet."

There was a collective gasp of shock in the room. "They were shooting at us!" shouted Webb, his eyes looking wild, his fists punching the air. "I screamed at Nat that we had to run in zig-zags so it would be harder for them to aim at us, but…"

"But what, Chris?" demanded Fox.

Webb looked round at all of the anxious faces surrounding him. "Nat didn't get the chance … he … he … was hit."

The word "No!" echoed around the room.

"He didn't stand a chance," whispered Webb. "He died instantly."

For a few moments, no one spoke. Emi and Adilson were crying. Corragio, Jobson, and Kelvin had their heads in their hands. Fox and Evans were white.

"I managed to make it to the road and flagged down a truck. I yelled at the driver to move and he stepped on it. He drove me straight here. I grabbed the nearest policeman and told him what had happened. I also told him I'd heard the kidnappers talking about going to some hideaway in Scotland. He called in some senior officers and relayed the whole story to them. They said they'd liaise with the Scottish police. I came straight here to break the news."

Webb hung his head. His eyes were red and sore, his body trembling.

The silence in the locker room engulfed everyone. It was Ian Fox who finally broke it. "I'm not sure the game can take place today."

Stan Evans touched the manager on the shoulder. "I've just had a message from the police inspector in charge of today's game. He knows what's going on, but says even though it's tragic what's happened to Nat, he can't cancel the game. There are nearly forty thousand people in here. The logistical issues and the potential for public disorder for emptying the stadium for a non-emergency isn't viable."

Ian Fox shook his head slightly. "OK," he said, "we'll play it, but I can tell you one thing—you won't be playing, Chris."

Webb straightened his shoulders, stopped trembling and locked eyes with his manager. "Of course I'm playing," he said, suddenly sounding resolute. "It's what Nat would have wanted. He was so excited about this game and it would be an insult to his memory if I pulled out. He'd be appalled if we didn't play."

Fox looked at Evans. Evans ran his fingers through his hair, took a very deep breath and blew out his cheeks.

The Wildman suddenly stood up, his eyes filled with fire. "Chris is right!" he shouted. "We'll play it and we'll WIN it for Nat! We'll mourn after the match."

Adilson got to his feet. "Yes!" he exclaimed, "We'll do it for Nat."

Seconds later, every single Rangers player was on his feet shouting agreement. Fox looked at Evans and scratched his cheek. "OK, lads," he called out, cutting off his players. "Go out there and do us all proud. Let's beat them and stay up with the big boys. We'll deal with everything else after the game. GO ON!"

The players moved as one, stomping out of the locker room toward the tunnel.

69

A Stadium in Shock

2:56 P.M.

Ian Fox had rushed to explain things to the referee and his assistants. Stan Evans was desperately trying to find Nat's father, after another fruitless bout of trying to reach him on his cell phone. Dave spotted him and gave him an excited wave. But his exhilarated expectation vanished the moment Dave saw Evans's somber expression.

Evans crouched down so his head was level with Dave's. "Mr. Levy," he began, "could I talk to you for a moment?"

"Sure," said Dave anxiously, "what can I do for you?"

"It would be better if you came with me," said Evans softly.

Dave immediately stood up. "What's going on?" he demanded, his face twisted with anxiety.

"I'll tell you inside," replied Evans, leading Dave to the nearest exit.

But they hadn't made it there when the two teams emerged from the tunnel. Dave, along with everyone else in the stadium, instantly noticed that the players were wearing black armbands.

Dave froze. "What's going on?" he repeated in a hoarse voice.

274

"Let's go inside," said Evans indicating the exit and placing a hand on Dave's arm. But Dave shook his hand off.

"I'm not going anywhere," he said, "until I know what's going on."

Wherever you looked, people were looking blank and asking the person next to them why the players were wearing armbands. There were shrugs and looks of confusion everywhere.

In the press box Ray Swinton shook his head. He was always on top of every story from the footballing world. If someone had died—even in the last few minutes, he'd have heard about it. He could also see that Chris Webb had either had a fight or had been injured in some kind of accident. The left side of his face was a mess. What on earth was going on?

Instead of going to their respective ends, the twenty-two players formed a large circle round the perimeter of the center circle and stood with their hands behind their backs.

Stan Evans tried to pull Dave toward the exit but he refused to budge, his expression resolute and terrified at the same time.

The Wildman held up a microphone. "Could I have your attention please?" he asked in a quiet but determined tone. All of the Rangers supporters instantly fell silent. Some of the Man United fans carried on singing, but their friends quieted them down and a few moments later the entire stadium was completely silent.

"Something tragic has happened today," said the Wildman, his voice booming out around the stadium. "One of our finest young players, a lad who has just broken into the first team—Nat Dixon—has been mercilessly gunned down and killed."

Horrified cries reverberated around the stadium.

Ray Swinton leaped to his feet.

In Block 4, Dave Levy collapsed as he let out a primal cry of agony. Stan Evans held him tight to stop him from falling.

"None of us knew him for long," continued the Wildman, his voice faltering, tears sliding down his cheeks. "But he was a totally dedicated player, someone with an incredibly bright future in the game. It is impossible to convey the depths of shock and sadness that run through our entire club, but in spite of our grief, the players and the manager felt that playing this game would be a fitting tribute to his memory."

Dave's body was heaving with pain as he cried out again and again.

"Football, as we all know, is just a game," went on the Wildman. "No one lives or dies by it. But someone has died today, and in the minutes and hours and days after this game, we will pay our proper respects to the memory of Nat Dixon. All of our thoughts go out to his father at this moment and we would ask you all to observe a minute's silence with us."

An Explosive Revelation

The minute began and the entire Ivy Stadium fell silent aside from the wounded cries of Nat's father.

But thirty seconds into the minute's silence there were sudden gasps by the mouth of the tunnel. The gasps turned into cries, which transformed into shouts, cheers, and yells. Applause started in the seats next to the tunnel and spread around the stadium like a bush fire. In a few moments, the whole place was ringing out with a deafening show of amazement and joy.

Everyone was on their feet. Everyone was screaming. Because there, running out onto the field, was Nat Dixon.

Dave stopped sobbing as he stared in disbelief at the figure racing across the turf.

Emi and Kelvin were the first of the Rangers players to move. They turned away from the center circle, as if in slow motion, but then exploded into real time as they sprinted toward Nat. Adilson was next, followed by Corragio, Jobson, Young, and the Wildman. Nat was completely mobbed. The only two Rangers players who didn't move were Steve Townsend and Chris Webb.

Webb looked as if he'd just been caught in the headlights of a Mack truck that was bearing down on him. He was unable to move. Three police officers had run onto the field just behind Nat. They grabbed Webb, cuffed him, and dragged him away. His legs wobbled, and for a second it looked like he was going to crash to the ground, but he stayed on his feet and was led into the tunnel and out of sight.

On the opposite side of the stadium Nat's dad was flying down the steps in Block 4. He had never run so fast or with such purpose. His heart felt like it was about to explode. He vaulted over the low wall at the front of the block and ran across the sandy track toward the field.

Two ushers blocked his path.

"STOP!" one of them shouted, pointing to a sign stating it was illegal to go onto the field. But Stan Evans was running right behind Dave.

"It's OK," shouted Evans, "let him on!"

The ushers hesitated, but seeing it was Stan Evans issuing the order they stepped out of the way. Dave jumped up onto the field and began running toward the cluster of players gathered around his son. When he reached the group, he fought through the melee.

As the players realized who it was, they parted. Nat saw his dad's elated face and a split second later, Dave threw his arms round Nat, nearly squeezing the life out of him.

"I thought you were dead!" shouted Dave through his sobs of joy.

"I know!" yelled Nat, laughing and crying at the same time and hugging him back.

The whole stadium was going wild—the Ivy had never

witnessed scenes like this. In the press box, Ray Swinton looked totally bewildered. Talk about not picking up on a huge story—how had he missed this one? And what was actually happening out there?

"I think we need to start the match." Ian Fox had a hand on Dave's shoulder. A couple of senior policemen were lurking in the background. Dave nodded and released Nat.

"Good luck today, Mr. Fox," he said. "We're all counting on you."

"I know," replied Fox. "My players are going to give it everything. That's all I can ask for. We'll talk afterward."

"Definitely," Dave nodded. He looked at Nat one more time. "Go for it, buddy!" He grinned, wiping the tears off his cheeks with the back of his hand. "We'll have time to talk after the game."

Fox led Dave and Nat toward the technical area. "You're on, Graham!" shouted Fox at his reserve goalie who, along with every other player, had no idea what was going on.

"Nat, you're on the bench," said Fox. "And I'd like you to sit just behind us," he added, gently nudging Dave toward a seat right behind the technical area.

The referee and his two assistants had a hurried conversation with the two senior police officers and then sprang into action.

The first assistant ran to the left sideline. The second assistant and the referee strode over to the center circle, where all of the players were congregated, discussing the most bizarre incident any of them had ever experienced.

"You won't be needing those," said the ref, pointing to the black armbands. All twenty-two players pulled off their armbands and handed them to the second assistant. When he'd collected them, he ran to the right sideline and handed the armbands over to an usher.

The referee called the Wildman and Harry Granger, the Man United captain, forward. He pulled out a coin and looked at the Wildman.

"Your call, Mr. Duffy," said the ref.

"Heads," said the Wildman, staring dispassionately at Granger.

The ref flipped the coin and caught it. "Heads it is!"

"We'll keep things the way they are," said the Wildman. "We'll attack the Shipper End in the second half."

"Fine by me," Granger replied.

The ref placed the ball on the center circle and looked at his assistants, who both indicated they were ready. The ref put the whistle into his mouth and blew.

The most crucial ninety minutes of Rangers' history had just begun.

The Match

Fox sat down next to Nat as Granger took the center and passed it to Man United's playmaker, Geraldo.

"I don't think you should play any part in this one, son," said Fox quietly. "You've been through what sounds like a terrible ordeal. I think you need to sit it out."

Nat glared at Fox. "Why do you think I made it back here before three o'clock, boss?" he snapped. "I'm fine, I'm ready, and if you ask me to go on, I'm totally up for it. Don't make me miss it because you feel sorry for me!"

Fox sighed very deeply and tutted under his breath. "OK," he conceded reluctantly, "but I'll only use you if I have to."

"Thanks, boss." Nat grinned, his eyes quickly turning back to the game, as Geraldo skipped past a couple of Rangers tackles.

Evans had given Nat a sandwich and a drink; combined with adrenaline, they gave him some energy. It had been ages since he had eaten. But it was almost unbearable for Nat to watch the first half.

Man United were all over Rangers. Their passing, dribbling, and shooting were in a different class. When Geraldo floated a curling thirty-sixth-minute free kick into the top right corner of the Rangers goal, Nat and the thirty thousand Rangers fans fell totally silent. Then five minutes before the break, Harry Granger rose above the Rangers defense and smashed in a powerful header. Rangers 0, Manchester United 2. Game over for Rangers?

There was worse to come. The Rangers fans and players groaned when they heard the other teams' half-time scores. Sunderland were losing 1–0 to Aston Villa. This was good. But Wigan were beating Spurs 1–0 and Bolton were tied 0–0 with Arsenal. The current state of the bottom of the table made agonizing reading.

Wigan	33 points
Bolton	31 points
Hatton Rangers	28 points
Sunderland	27 points

It looked as if Rangers were done for; relegation and the end of the club seemed inevitable.

In the locker room at half-time, Ian Fox went crazy. He was like an out-of-control toy robot, his hands jerking all over the place, his eyes crimson with fury.

"Don't you guys realize what's at stake here?" he screamed. "This isn't just about my future and your future. This is about the future of every person who pays your salaries! You're letting them all down. If you want your career in soccer to end today, then carry on playing like you did in the first half! If you want to stay in the game, then *up* your game a million-fold!"

The atmosphere in the room after Fox's rant was electric. Faces that had looked dejected a minute before were suddenly full of resolve. The Wildman went around to every player, shouting encouragement, desperately attempting to restore their self-belief.

Rangers came out for the second half a totally different team. They were playing for their survival and realized that nervousness would not help their cause. At fifty-eight minutes, Adilson pumped the ball into the penalty area. Paolo Corragio took it on his chest and hit it on the way down. The United goalie, Finn Pedersen, got a hand on it, but it smashed into the back of the net. The Rangers players and fans went so wild you'd be forgiven for thinking they'd just won the Premier League and the FA Cup at the same moment.

Higher and higher flew the Rangers flags and banners as the crowd roared the team on. United had a couple of half-chances, but then at sixty-six minutes Rangers broke. Emi found Sacrois with a beautifully weighted pass. Sacrois turned a United defender and found Steve Townsend racing through into the box. He was onside. Nat along with everyone else stood up, willing Townsend to bury it. But Townsend scuffed his shot and the ball rolled weakly into the arms of Pedersen.

"WHAT WAS THAT?" screamed Fox, his eyes bulging with fury—a sentiment shared by the vast majority of the crowd. A few seconds later, Fox turned to Nat. "Get changed," he said in a steely voice. "You're going on."

Sixty-seven minutes. This wasn't going to be some fleeting five-minute run-out. This was sixty-seven minutes! Twenty-three minutes to go, plus time added on!

Nat quickly pulled off his jacket and started running along the sidelines. Fox told the assistant referee of the change and a few moments later the assistant held up his board. The ref spotted it and ordered the substitution to take place.

"Substitution for Rangers," boomed the loudspeaker. "Coming off, number nine, Steve Townsend, who will be replaced by number thirty-three, Nat Dixon!"

The tumultuous applause that greeted his name amazed Nat. Were they just cheering because they had thought he was dead, or were they showing their appreciation of his talent? Either way, it didn't matter. There were twenty-three minutes of the game to go—twenty-three minutes in which Rangers had to score twice or face going down.

Townsend marched off the field and threw his shirt on the ground in disgust. He directed a hate-filled stare at Fox and stamped off into the tunnel, uttering a string of curses on his way.

12

All Action

Nat was involved almost immediately. Kelvin found him with a pass. He evaded a Man United challenge and passed the ball to Sacrois, whose shot went wide. A few minutes later, he stole the ball off Geraldo, and flicked the ball to Dean Jobson, who returned the pass. Nat saw a tiny opening and whacked the ball. It was a good effort and Pedersen had to dive to catch it.

"Well done, son!" yelled the Wildman approvingly. "I want more of the same!"

The Wildman's praise buoyed Nat up and he had another shooting opportunity five minutes later. Unselfishly, though, he passed it to Dennis Jensen, who was in a better position. Jensen's shot was low and fast, but it was straight at Pedersen, who grabbed it gratefully.

As the minutes went by, the tension in the stadium was becoming unbearable. The Rangers fans were shouting themselves hoarse and their team was mounting attack after attack, with no success.

But then, in the eighty-third minute, Nat received the ball on the right side of the United penalty area.

He made as if he were going to run toward the goal line and was tracked by a Man United defender. But he dummied a shift to the right and nutmegged the player. With the ball at his feet, he sprinted into the penalty area and, as Harry Granger made a lunge for him, Nat skipped out of the way and lofted the ball over to the other side of the area, where Adilson was waiting. The Brazilian feinted a shot, causing two United players to throw themselves leftward. Then, very calmly, he drove the ball goalward. It evaded the sprawling United keeper and struck home. GOAL!!!

Adilson ran straight toward Nat and threw his arm around his neck. The other Rangers players leaped on top of them.

"GET OFF THEM!" yelled the Wildman urgently, "We're still dead in the water!"

This clarion call roused the team and they quickly ran back to their own half for the United kick-off. United had decided to play the game out for a tie and they took the ball back deep into Rangers' half and started making short passes by one of the corner flags. The tactic was met with resounding boos and whistles by the Rangers fans.

The Wildman and Kelvin weren't buying it either. They crashed into the midst of the United players and claimed the ball. Kelvin whacked it to Sacrois, who beat his man and centered it to Dennis Jensen.

"LAST MINUTE!" they heard Stan Evans yelling.

Jensen stroked it on to Nat. There were three United players running toward him, including the giant frame of Harry Granger. But with an amazing display of ball control and agility, Nat dribbled around all three and found himself inside the area and bearing down on the United goal.

The screams of the Rangers fans seemed to recede into the background as Nat raced toward Finn Pedersen, who was already shaping his body to narrow the angle. It was a shooting situation Nat had found himself in thousands of times. All he had to do was curl the ball to the right of the goalie and it would spin into the goal. Even though Pedersen was a huge guy, Nat was certain he could bend it past him. He pulled back his right foot to shoot, but was suddenly knocked off balance and went crashing onto the turf. The ball trickled into Pedersen's hands.

Nat spun round and saw Harry Granger holding his arms in the air and protesting his innocence. "I GOT THE BALL!" he shouted at the ref. The ref immediately reached into his pocket and showed Granger the red card.

"NO WAY!" shouted Granger, "I played the ball!"

But the ref waved his protests away and kept his arm straight. Granger shook his head several times and then began the trek off the field.

The ref paused for an agonizing second and then pointed to the penalty spot.

13

The Endgame

The crowd noise was so loud it was hard to hear anything on the field, even if someone was standing right next to you. Adilson usually took the penalties, but he was rooted to the spot, fear on his face. "I can't do it," he mouthed at the Wildman. "I missed the last one. I can't do it. I'm sorry."

The Wildman took a deep breath. "I'll take it, then," he said, picking up the ball and starting to walk to the penalty spot.

Nat reacted instantly. He ran up to the Wildman. "Let me take it," he said. "I've taken loads of penalties in my time. You're a defender. No disrespect, but I'll have a better chance."

The Wildman looked at him with a mix of astonishment and admiration. "I can't let this ruin your life," he said. "The responsibility's too massive."

"I mean it," said Nat. "Please, let me take it."

The Wildman stopped just short of the penalty spot and looked around at his teammates. Emi and Kelvin nodded, and they were followed by the rest of the team.

"Are you a hundred percent sure?" the Wildman asked Nat.

Nat nodded.

The Wildman handed Nat the ball.

Nat rolled the ball in his hands, knelt down, and placed it very carefully on the penalty spot. A couple of United defenders started to walk over to him with the intention of intimidating him, but the Wildman stepped in their way.

Suddenly, extra mayhem erupted in the stadium. Spurs had scored midway through the second half of their game against Wigan, and then had got a last-minute goal to win 2–1. Arsenal had scored three second-half goals to beat Bolton. If Rangers' penalty was converted and the three other scores stayed the same, Rangers would survive!

Nat blocked out the encouraging yelling of the Rangers fans and the harsh whistles of the Manchester United fans. He stared at the goal, where the muscular Pedersen was raising his arms and looking like an oversized fluorescent green bat, and for a few seconds he lost his nerve: *Why on earth did I volunteer to take this shot?*

He silently said a prayer—thank you, God, for saving my life back there—and please, please, help me score this one goal. For the team.

Determination flooded through him. Admittedly, he'd never taken a penalty against one of the world's best goalkeepers, but the technique was always the same. If you aimed for one of the top corners, no keeper, however big they were, could possibly reach the ball. It was very risky because it was easy to miss, but Nat's nerve held.

He took several deep breaths and a few steps back from the ball. He looked around quickly. All of the other players were gathered outside the area, even Graham Dalston, who'd run the entire length of the field in a desperate gesture to add an extra body to the Rangers attack for the dying seconds of the game.

Nat turned back to face the ball and waited. It seemed like a century before the ref blew his whistle.

He counted to three in his head and began his run. Pedersen's arms had dropped now. The psychological game was over. Nat made excellent contact with the ball. It rose and crashed straight toward the top corner to Pedersen's left. The keeper dived the wrong way. For a second it looked as if the ball would fly above the goal. But then it dipped and it seemed as if it would go straight in.

But it smashed against the crossbar. An enormous groan of agony erupted in the stadium and Nat's heart plummeted. Disaster!

But he was already sprinting forward ahead of the rest of the pack. As the ball dropped onto the goal line, Pedersen adjusted his footing and made a desperate lunge for it. But it was a couple of inches beyond his grasp. Nat flung himself at the ball, threw out his right leg and prodded it into the goal. It crashed over Pedersen's outstretched arm and slammed into the back of the net.

As Nat was mobbed by his teammates, the Rangers fans went berserk, and a crushed Finn Pedersen scooped the ball out of his net, the referee blew his whistle.

Full-time. Hatton Rangers 3, Manchester United 2.

14

Aftermath

The following ten minutes were completely crazy. The entire Rangers bench ran onto the field, where several fans who had managed to evade ushers, security, and police officers joined them. The United players sank to the ground in disappointment—it was a terrible result to end the season.

Pierre Sacrois and Kelvin hoisted Nat onto their shoulders and thousands of phone cameras clicked as fans recorded an image of the teenager who had just ensured Hatton Rangers' Premiership survival.

Once the police had cleared away the over-zealous fans, the Rangers team and staff spent twenty minutes doing a circuit of the field, stopping at each section and applauding the fans while posing for photos.

During the celebrations, the Wildman put an arm round Nat's shoulders. "Unless you play for one of the big teams, it's not often you get moments like this in your career," he said. "So enjoy it, Nat—you deserve it!"

Nat jumped up, pounded the air with his fists and yelled along with his teammates. It felt incredible to be here.

Finally, after another five minutes of celebrations in front of the technical area, the players and staff left the field and headed down into the tunnel.

A woman dressed in a stylish beige pantsuit, with a Rangers badge on her jacket, approached Nat.

"Hi Nat, I'm Helen Aldershot—publicity. We've been flooded with requests for interviews with you! There's the BBC, ITV, Sky Sports, and at least six other TV companies, plus about thirty newspapers and magazines and five web-based services. How many of those do you think you can fit in?"

She looked at him expectantly.

"At this stage there's only one press person I'm willing to talk to," he replied.

"Oh," she said, the disappointment clear on her face. "Who's that?"

"Ray Swinton from the *Sunday Crest*," Nat replied.

*

Five miles away from the raucous scenes at the Ivy Stadium, a black station wagon sat in an empty side street, its single passenger massaging his temples, his body shaking with rage and shock. The person on the other end of the phone was letting his feelings be known; Knight had just blown a substantial sum of his hard-earned money.

"I know," said Knight hoarsely. "How was I to know the Dixon kid would get involved? I'm sorry, it's just very, very bad luck."

The caller screamed at Knight again, and Knight ended the call. He called Tanner again, but for the twenty-first time it went straight to voicemail.

Knight clenched his fists as he considered his future. He'd just lost his three investors millions of pounds. Yes, they had deep pockets, but it was a big enough sum to be noticed. There was no way they were going to let this thing go without a fight.

*

In the Rangers locker room, the celebrations were continuing. Everyone was singing and/or dancing, except for Steve Townsend, who was packing his bag. But when he made to leave he found his path blocked by Ian Fox.

"Can you get out of my way?" demanded Townsend testily.

The shouting and cheering suddenly subsided as everyone turned to check out this face-off.

"I said, will you move to the side!" Townsend snarled.

"In a word, no!" snapped Fox. "Not until I tell you that you've just played your last game for Rangers."

Several of the players' mouths fell open.

"I'm sick of your gambling, but most of all I'm sick of your negative attitude!" shouted Fox. "You're poison and have been for ages. You bring your negative vibes into the club every day and I don't want you anywhere near Rangers ever again. And don't go thinking you'll be getting any compensation because I've been keeping track of all of your gambling sprees and will be more than happy to talk about them to any other club who might be stupid enough to show an interest in you. If you keep your mouth shut, I'll do the same and I'll let you go on a free transfer this summer. That's the only offer on the table, so take it or leave it."

Townsend looked as if he was about to shout something back at Fox, but changed his mind, barged past the Rangers manager and stormed out of the door. The action was met with cheers and applause from every other member of the squad.

At that moment, Stan Evans got a call on his cell phone. He put his hand over his ear so he could hear the caller over the joyous sounds of singing and screaming. When the call was over, he walked over to Nat.

"It's Helen Aldershot from publicity," he said, his brow knitted with suspicion and concern. "Apparently you've agreed to talk to Ray Swinton from the *Sunday Crest*? She says he's over in one of the conference rooms waiting for you."

"Thanks, Stan," replied Nat.

"I think I should come with you," said Evans, putting a hand on Nat's shoulder.

"Don't worry, Stan." Nat smiled. "I'll be fine. I've got a score to settle with him. I promise you I know what I'm doing."

"Are you sure?" Evans asked, looking doubtful. "Ray Swinton is a wily old operator. He coaxes things out of people that they'd sworn never to tell anyone."

"I'll be fine," Nat repeated. "I know what I'm doing."

Evans made a face but withdrew his hand. "Good luck, Nat," he said. "Call me immediately if you need me."

Nat nodded and headed out of the room.

Filing the Story

"So, let me get this straight."

Ray Swinton and Nat had the conference room to themselves.

"Chris Webb was going to throw the game, allowing a consortium of crooks who had bet on a Rangers loss, to collect millions of pounds."

"Correct." Nat nodded. "They bet on him letting in three goals during a certain time frame and he was going to deliver the goods. Only problem is, he didn't play, so the bets were completely wasted."

"Someone out there isn't going to be very happy, then, are they?" mused Swinton.

"You could say that," agreed Nat.

"How did you find out about this plan?"

"I stumbled into Webb's meeting completely by accident. They caught me listening in and locked me up in a storeroom. Then the guy Webb was with, Tanner, punched Webb to make it look like he'd been attacked. I thought Tanner was going to shoot me, but they left me there to die."

"How did you get out of the storeroom?"

"I found an old can of furniture polish on a cleaning cart in the room. It was still about a quarter full. When

Tanner came in, I charged at him and sprayed it in his face. He started running around the room clutching his eyes. I also grabbed his phone from the table so he couldn't call Webb, or send anyone else after me."

"What happened to the gun?"

"He was still holding it. I realized if I made a lunge for it, I might get shot, so I ran while I could."

"And you reached the road?"

"Yeah, and the first truck I flagged down stopped. Tanner was back on my trail by then but I got away."

Swinton looked down at his copious notes. "So this Tanner guy was heading to Scotland?"

Nat shook his head. "That was just Webb's story to put the police off the scent. I heard them talking about Spain, so I passed that info on."

"This Tanner character sounds like a real tough guy," observed Swinton.

"Definitely." Nat shivered. "I was lucky to get out of there alive."

"This is great stuff," said Swinton, chewing his bottom lip. "It would make an incredible splash. Are you offering it to me on a totally exclusive basis? Photos, quotes, the lot?"

"It's all yours."

Swinton knitted the fingers of both hands together and mulled over everything Nat had told him.

"Come on, Ray," said Nat. "This is a far bigger story than your mad theory about me being only thirteen. You're going to go for it, right?"

16

Dash for Freedom

"Please ensure all your luggage is in the overhead lockers and, as we're preparing for take-off, please fasten your seatbelts."

Tanner clicked his seatbelt into place and pushed his seat back as far as it would go. He hated flying economy, but you took what you got with last-minute flights. He'd had to move quickly; the prospect of Knight and his investors coming after him wasn't a pleasant one. They'd all blame him for the disaster, but how was he to know the Dixon kid would find the spray and attack him? He adjusted his shades. He didn't want to arouse any suspicion, which he might if people saw his badly bloodshot and still raw eyes.

He had switched on the radio for the last five minutes of the Rangers vs. Man United game and had been staggered when he realized Webb wasn't even on the field. When Dixon scored with that last-gasp penalty it was as if the center of his body had been yanked out of the rest of it. He couldn't believe it! All that hard planning, not to mention hard cash, and the game had gone the wrong way.

He sighed and looked on the bright side. In an hour and a half he'd be in Spain: gorgeous weather, delicious food, and several associates who owed him favors and would be more than happy to hide him from prying eyes for a while, until the heat was off. Then he'd move on. Where would he go? He had a friend who ran a semi-legitimate property company in Croatia and a distant cousin who was operating *several credit-card scams in Australia. Either of those guys would help set him up. If necessary he wouldn't just get a new identity, he'd get a new face—you could buy one for a few grand.*

He felt the bulge in his jacket pocket. His stash of money was safely stowed there and he'd already wired the rest into an offshore account on the Cayman Islands. Money wasn't going to be a problem. He closed his eyes as the captain started the engine and began taxiing toward the runway.

The Agreement

"So?" asked Nat eagerly. "Do we have a deal, Ray? Will you go for the Webb story?"

Swinton took a deep breath. "I think you've convinced me," he replied.

There was silence in the conference room for a few moments. It was Nat who broke it. "So how old am I?" he asked.

Swinton paused for a few moments and then replied. "Sixteen." He nodded. "Just another sixteen-year-old who's broken into the Premier League."

"Nothing newsworthy about that, is there, Ray?" asked Nat.

"Nothing newsworthy at all … unless you get a call-up for the England squad."

Nat laughed. "There is one other thing," he said.

"Yes?"

"I want you to phone your contact in Brazil and tell them they've got it completely wrong. I'm not the kid they met out there; you've checked all your sources, and the truth is I did come from the US."

"No problem," said Swinton. "Now, about an opening quote for the story…"

Fenced In

Tanner woke up as the plane suddenly juddered to a halt. Passengers were jolted forward and several young kids started crying.

"What's going on?" asked the woman sitting next to Tanner.

A couple of seconds later, two armed police officers boarded the plane and started striding down the aisle. Several passengers screamed.

Tanner gulped and stood up. The officers were rapidly advancing toward him. In a panic he spun around, but was faced with another two officers approaching him from behind. He was caught—trapped.

"Put your hands on your head!" barked one of the officers.

By now, every passenger was staring at the unfolding drama. One man raised his phone to take a photo, but was glared at by one of the policemen and withdrew the gadget instantly.

Tanner cursed his bad luck as the officers neared him. The Dixon kid must have put the police onto him; either that or Knight had snitched on him—attempting to set him up as the fall guy. Slowly he raised his arms in the air.

The first officer to reach him slapped handcuffs on his

wrists and the four of them started ushering him down the aisle. Tanner felt despair in the pit of his stomach. His vision of a comfortable semi-retirement in Spain had just gone up in smoke.

Close Season

Ray Swinton switched off his voice recorder and picked up his bag. He reached out his hand and Nat shook it. Then they stood up, walked across the room, and went through the door. A short way down the hall stood Fox, Evans, and Nat's dad.

"I'll be in touch," said Swinton to Nat, nodding a greeting to the three waiting figures before hurrying off down the corridor.

Nat walked over to them. Dave grabbed Nat by the shoulders and squeezed him.

"How did it go?" he asked nervously. "Did he give you a hard time?"

Nat laughed. "It'll be fine. I gave him an exclusive on the Chris Webb situation. You don't need to worry about him."

His dad sighed with relief and then a proud smile spread across his face. "It's easy to forget the game in all of the other stuff that's gone on," he said, "but I just wanted to say that you were brilliant on the field. The run that earned Rangers a penalty was first class, wasn't it?"

"As good as any of the top players." Evans beamed. "If we can build up your upper-body strength and get you playing for the first team regularly, there's no saying what you'll be able to do."

"Mr. Fox?" asked Dave.

Ian Fox thought for a few moments. "I'm never one to get carried away with gushing praise, as I'm sure you're all aware. You did well today, Nat, but don't forget that, however significant the result is, it was still a sub's appearance for the last section of a game. You haven't even played a full half for us, so let's not get too carried away."

Nat sighed but nodded his acceptance. He'd made a small start in the world of Premier League football; he had a long, long way to go.

"We're going to leave you," said Fox. "We need to start planning next season's campaign and see if Mr. Pritchard is amenable to buying a couple of new players, seeing as the Premier League TV revenue will still be coming in."

Fox and Evans both shook hands with Dave and then with Nat.

"We'll give you a ring tonight," said Fox, "and get the whole story off you then, if that's OK?"

"Definitely," replied Nat.

"Then we'll see you for pre-season training in three weeks." Stan Evans winked at them. "What are you going to do with your break?"

Nat shrugged his shoulders. "I have no idea," he replied. "Probably sleep and watch TV."

The three adults laughed.

"Stay clear of injuries," advised Fox, as he and Evans turned and walked off down the hall.

Stepping Out

Nat and his dad stood alone, staring at each other.

"This whole thing is completely unbelievable, isn't it?" Dave grinned. "I mean, we've only been back in the country for just over a month and all this has happened. You're playing professional football for Rangers, Nat! I still don't know what you got caught up in back there. What a *ganze megillah*! But thank God, the most important thing is that you're OK."

"I know," replied Nat, "there's so much stuff crammed into my head—I think it's going to explode."

Dave laughed, but a few seconds later, his expression suddenly became serious.

"You know what, buddy?" he said, lowering his voice. "However little interest she had in football, your mum would have been bursting with pride today."

Nat felt a lump in his throat as he looked at his dad.

If only she'd been here to see it.

The silence would have continued if it wasn't for the appearance of the publicity woman, Helen Aldershot.

"Sorry to interrupt you gents," she said, smiling, "but I really think you need to go outside soon, Nat. There are a lot of people out there waiting to see you."

"Me?" asked Nat.

Helen nodded emphatically. "You just saved the club from relegation!" She laughed. "They want to thank you!"

Nat shook his head in amazement. This morning he'd been a tiny bit-player in the drama of Rangers' survival battle and now he had his own crowd of well-wishers!

"After you," said Helen, ushering them down the hall. They took a couple of turns, went down some stairs and finally reached the lobby in front of the stadium's main entrance. Nat gulped when he saw the huge crowd outside, waving banners and scarves and holding up their phones. They started cheering and whistling when they caught sight of Nat.

"This is crazy," he said in shock.

"Crazy or not," said Helen, "you just need to go out there, sign a few autographs, and pose for some photos. Ten minutes max and I'll come out and get you in. There are plenty of security guards out there to make sure you don't get mobbed!"

Nat turned to his dad.

"Go for it." Dave smiled. "I'll be waiting here for you. We'll go out for a celebration meal tonight, how about that?"

"Nice one!" Nat beamed.

Helen Aldershot walked across to the glass door. "Are you ready?" she asked, looking back.

Nat nodded and stepped toward her. The crowd started screaming louder and more wildly.

"OK." She smiled, pulling open the door. "You're on."

Nat took a deep breath and walked outside.

About the Author

As a child Jonny Zucker devoured any stories about football or footballers, and was especially influenced by a book called *Goalkeepers are Different* by Brian Glanville. He set his heart on being a writer and in particular, writing a novel that combined a football story with a thriller plot. *Striker Boy* is that book. On the path to becoming a writer Jonny worked as a primary school teacher, FA-qualified football coach and stand-up comedian.

Sadly, Jonny passed away in 2016. He was a loving husband and an adoring father.